JATAKA
TALES

By
Rajesh Kavassery

YOUNG KIDS PRESS

(An imprint of Sura College of Competition)

- Chennai • Tirunelveli • Ernakulam
- Thiruvananthapuram • Bengalooru

© PUBLISHERS
JATAKA TALES
by
Rajesh Kavassery

This Edition : February, 2016
Size : 1/8 Crown
Pages : 128

ISBN : 81-7478-955-3
Code: G 59

YOUNG KIDS PRESS
[An imprint of Sura College of Competition]

Head Office: 1620, 'J' Block, 16th Main Road, Anna Nagar,
Chennai - 600 040. Phones: 044-26162173, 26161099.

Branches :
- KAP Complex, I Floor, 20, Trivandrum Road,
  Tirunelveli - 627 002. Phone : 0462-4200557

- 35/1465, Kochaneth Tower, Ground Floor,
  Ratnam Lane, South Janatha Road, Palarivattom,
  Ernakulam - 682 025. Phones: 0484-3205797, 2535636

- TC 28/2816, Sriniketan, Kuthiravattam Road,
  Thiruvananthapuram - 695 001. Phone: 0471-4063864

- 3638/A, 4th Cross, Opp. to Malleswaram Railway Station,
  Gayathri Nagar, Back gate of Subramaniya Nagar,
  Bengalooru - 560 021. Phone: 080-23324950

Sri Maruthi Graphics, Chennai - 600 032 and Published by
V.V.K.Subhuraj for Young Kids Press [An imprint of Sura College of Competition]
1620, 'J' Block, 16th Main Road, Anna Nagar, Chennai - 600 040.
Phones: 26162173, 26161099. Fax: (91) 44-26162173.
e-mail: enquiry@surabooks.com; website: www.surabooks.com

02 16 1000

CONTENTS

Jataka Tales

1. THE HYPOCRITICAL HOLY MAN

Once upon a time, there was a crooked holy man. He wore nothing but rags, had long matted hair, and relied on a little village to support him. But he was sneaky and tricky. He only pretended to give up attachment to the everyday world. He was a phoney holy man.

A wealthy man living in the village wanted to earn merit by doing good deeds. So he had a simple little temple built in the nearby forest for the holy man to live in. He also fed him the finest foods from his own home.

He thought this holy man with matted hair was sincere and good, one who would not do anything unwholesome. Since he was afraid of bandits, he took his family fortune of 100 gold coins to the little temple. He buried it under the ground and said to the holy man, "Venerable One, please look after this, it is my family fortune."

The holy man replied, "There's no need to worry about such things with people like me. We holy ones have given up attachment to the ordinary world. We have no greed or desire to obtain the possessions of others."

"Very well, Venerable One," said the man. He left thinking himself very wise indeed, to trust such a good holy man.

However, the wicked holy man thought, "Aha! This treasure of 100 gold coins is enough for me to live on for the rest of my life! I will never have to work or beg again!" So a few days later he dug up the gold and secretly buried it near the roadside.

The next day he went to the wealthy villager's home for lunch as usual. After eating his fill he said, "Most honourable gentleman, I have lived here supported by you for a long time. But holy ones who have given up the world are not supposed to become too attached to one village or supporter. It would make a holy man like me impure! Therefore, kindly permit me to humbly go on my way."

The man pleaded with him again and again not to go, but it was useless. "Go then, Venerable Sir," he agreed at last. He went with him as far as the boundary of the village and left him there.

After going on a short way himself, the phoney holy man thought, "I must make absolutely sure that this stupid villager does not suspect me. He trusts me so much that he will believe anything. So I will deceive him with a clever trick!" He stuck a blade of dry grass in his matted hair and went back.

When he saw him returning, the wealthy villager asked, "Venerable One, why have you come back?"

He replied, "Dear friend, this blade of grass from the thatched roof of your house has stuck in my hair. It is most unwholesome and impure for a holy one such as myself to 'take what is not given'."

The amazed villager said, "Think nothing of it, Your Reverence. Please put it down and continue on your way. Venerable ones such as you do not even take a blade of grass that belongs to another. How marvellous! How exalted you are, the purest of the holy. How lucky I was to be able to support you!" More trusting than ever, he bowed respectfully and sent him on his way again.

It just so happened that the Bodhisattva was living the life of a trader at that time. He was in the midst of a trading trip when he stopped overnight at the village. He had overheard the entire conversation between the villager and the 'purest of the holy'. He thought, "That sounds ridiculous! This man must have stolen something far more valuable than the blade of dry grass, he has made such a big show of returning to its rightful owner."

The trader asked the wealthy villager, "Friend, did you perhaps give anything to this holy looking man for safekeeping?"

"Yes friend," he replied, "I trusted him to guard my family fortune of 100 gold coins."

"I advise you to go and see if they are where you left them," said the trader.

Suddenly worried, he ran to the forest temple, dug up the ground, and found his treasure gone. He ran back to the trader and said, "It has been stolen!"

"Friend," he replied, "No one but that so-called holy man could have taken it. Let's catch him and get your treasure back."

They both chased after him as fast as they could. When they caught up with him they made him tell where he had hidden the money. They went to the hiding place by the roadside and dug up the buried treasure.

Looking at the gleaming gold the Bodhisattva said, "You hypocritical holy man. You spoke well those beautiful words, admired by all, that one is not to 'take what is not given'. You hesitated to leave with even a blade of grass that didn't belong to you. But it was so easy for you to steal a hundred gold coins!" After ridiculing the way he had acted, he advised him to change his ways for his own good.

🐘 🐘 🐘

2. THE PRIEST AND THE SNAKE

Once upon a time, there lived an intelligent man. He was the adviser priest of King Brahmadatta. He was generous with his wealth and knowledge, holding nothing back. People thought of him as a kind and good person.

By practising the Five Training Steps, he trained his mind to avoid the five unwholesome actions. He discovered that giving up each unwholesome action made him better off in its own way:

- ♦ destroying life, since you have to kill part of yourself in order to kill someone else;
- ♦ taking what is not given, since this makes the owner angry at you;
- ♦ doing wrong in sexual ways, since this leads to the pain of jealousy and envy;
- ♦ speaking falsely, since you can't be true to yourself and false to another at the same time;
- ♦ losing your mind from alcohol, since then you might hurt yourself by doing the other four.

Seeing how he lived, King Brahmadatta thought, "This is truly a good man."

The priest was curious to learn more about the value of goodness. He thought, "The King honours and respects me more than his other priests. But I wonder what it is about me that he really respects most. Is it my nationality, my noble birth or family wealth? Is it my great learning and vast knowledge? Or is it because of my goodness? I must find the answer to this."

Therefore, he decided to perform an experiment in order to answer his question. He would pretend to be a thief!

On the next day, when he was leaving the palace, he went by the royal coin maker. He was stamping out coins from gold. The good priest, not intending to keep it, took a coin and continued walking out of the palace. Because the money maker admired the famous priest highly, he remained sitting and said nothing.

On the following day the make-believe thief took two gold coins. Again the royal coin maker did not protest.

Finally, on the third day, the King's favourite priest grabbed a whole handful of gold coins. This time the money maker didn't care about the priest's position or reputation. He cried out, "This is the third time you have robbed his majesty, the King." Holding onto him, he shouted, "I've caught the thief who robs the King! I've caught the thief who robs the King! I've caught the thief who robs the King!"

Suddenly a crowd of people came running in, yelling, "Aha! You pretended to be better than us! An example of goodness!" They slapped him, tied his hands behind his back, and hauled him off to the King.

But on their way, they happened to go by some snake charmers. They were entertaining some bystanders from the King's court with a poisonous cobra. They held him by the tail and neck, and coiled him around their necks to show how brave they were.

The tied up prisoner said to them, "Please be careful! Don't grab that cobra by the tail. Don't grab him by his neck. And don't coil that poisonous snake around your own necks. He may bite you and bring your lives to a sudden end!"

The snake charmers said, "You ignorant priest, you don't understand this cobra. He is well-mannered and very good indeed. He is not bad like you! You are a thief who has stolen from the King. Because of your wickedness and criminal behaviour, you are being carried off with your hands tied behind your back. But there's no need to tie up a snake who is good!"

The priest thought, "Even a poisonous cobra, who doesn't bite or harm anyone, is given the name 'good'. In truth, goodness is the quality people admire most in the world!"

When they arrived at the throne room, the King asked, "What is this, my children?"

They replied, "This is the thief who stole from your royal treasury."

The King said, "Then punish him according to the law."

The adviser priest said, "My lord King, I am no thief!"

"Then why did you take gold coins from the palace?" asked the King.

The priest explained, "I have done this only as an experiment, to test why it is you honour and respect me more than others. Is it because of my family background and wealth, or my great knowledge? Because of those things, I was able to get away with taking one or two gold coins. Or do you respect my goodness most of all? It is clear that by grabbing a handful of coins I no longer had the name 'good'. This alone turned respect into disgrace!

"Even a poisonous cobra, who doesn't harm anyone, is called 'good'. There is no need for any other title!"

To emphasize the lesson he had learned, the wise priest recited:

"High birth and wealth and even knowledge vast, I find, are less admired than goodness is, by humankind."

The King pardoned his most valuable adviser priest.

He asked to be allowed to leave the King's service in the ordinary world and become a forest monk. After refusing several times, the King eventually gave his permission.

The priest went to the Himalayas and meditated peacefully. When he died he was reborn in a heaven world.

3. THE PRIEST LUCKY CLOTH AND THE HOLY MAN

Once upon a time, the Bodhisattva was born into a high class family. When he grew up, he realized that his ordinary life could not give him lasting happiness. So he left everything behind and went to live in the Himalayas as a forest monk. He meditated and gained knowledge and peace of mind.

One day he decided to come down from the Himalayan forests to the city of Rajagaha. When he arrived he stayed overnight in the King's pleasure garden.

The next morning he went into the city to collect alms food. The King saw him and was pleased with his humble and dignified attitude. So he invited him to the palace. He offered him a seat and gave him the best food to eat. Then he invited him to live in the garden for good. The holy man agreed, and from then on he lived in the King's pleasure garden and had his meals in the King's palace.

At that time there was a priest in the city who was known as 'Lucky Cloth'. He used to predict good or bad luck by examining a piece of cloth.

It just so happened that he had a new suit of clothes. One day, after his bath, he asked his servant to bring the suit to him. The servant saw that it had been chewed slightly by mice, so he told the priest.

Lucky Cloth thought, "It is dangerous to keep in the house these clothes that have been chewed by mice. This is a sure sign of a curse that could destroy my home. Therefore, I can't even give them to my children or servants. The curse would still be in my house!

"In fact, I can't give these unlucky clothes to anyone. The only safe thing to do is to get rid of them once and for all. The best way to do that is to throw them in the corpse grounds, the place where dead bodies are put for wild animals to eat.

"But how can I do that? If I tell a servant to do it, desire will make him keep the clothes, and the curse will remain in my household. Therefore, I can trust this task only to my son."

He called his son to him and told all about the curse of the clothes that were slightly chewed by mice. He told

him not to even touch them with his hand. He was to carry them on a stick and go throw them in the corpse grounds. Then he must bathe from head to foot before returning home.

The son obeyed his father. When he arrived at the corpse grounds, carrying the clothes on a stick, he found the holy man sitting by the gate. When Lucky Cloth's son threw away the cursed suit, the holy man picked it up. He examined it and saw the tiny teeth marks made by the mice. But since they could hardly be noticed, he took the suit with him back to the pleasure garden.

After bathing thoroughly, his son told Priest Lucky Cloth what had happened. He thought, "This cursed suit of clothes will bring great harm to the King's favourite holy man. I must warn him."

So he went to the pleasure garden and said. "Holy One! Please throw away the unlucky cloth you have taken! It is cursed and will bring harm to you!"

But the holy man replied, "No, no, what others throw away in the corpse grounds is a blessing to me! We forest meditators are not seers of good and bad luck. All kinds of Buddhas and Enlightened Beings have given up superstitions about luck. Anyone who is wise should do the same. No one knows the future!"

Hearing about the truly wise and enlightened ones made Priest Lucky Cloth see how foolish he had been. From then on he gave up his many superstitions and followed the teachings of the humble holy man.

4. THE TWO MOTHERS

A woman, carrying her child, went to a tank. First she bathed her child, and then put on her upper garment and descended into the water to bathe herself.

Then a Yaksha, seeing the child, had a craving to eat it. And taking the form of a woman, she drew near, and asked the mother, "Friend, this is a very pretty child. Is it one of yours?" And when she was told it was, she asked if she might nurse it. And this being allowed, she nursed it a little, and then carried it off.

But when the mother saw this, she ran after her, and cried out, "Where are you taking my child to?" and caught hold of her.

The Yaksha boldly said, "Where did you get the child from? It is mine!" And so quarrelling, they passed the door of the future Buddha's Judgement Hall.

He heard the noise, sent for them, inquired into the matter, and asked them whether they would abide by his decision. And they agreed. Then he had a line drawn on the ground; and told the Yaksha to take hold of the child's arms, and the mother to take hold of its legs; and said, "The child shall be hers who drags him over the line."

But as soon as they pulled at him, the mother, seeing how he suffered, grieved as if her heart would break. And letting him go, she stood there weeping.

Then the future Buddha asked the bystanders, "Whose hearts are tender to babes? Those who have borne children, or those who have not?"

And they answered, "O Sire! The hearts of mothers are tender."

Then he said, "Who, think you, is the mother? She who has the child in her arms, or she who has let go?"

And they answered, "She who has let go is the mother."

And he said, "Then do you all think that the other was the thief?"

And they answered, "Sire! We cannot tell."

And he said, "Verily, this is a Yaksha, who took the child to eat it."

And he replied, "Because her eyes winked not, and were red, and she knew no fear, and had no pity, I knew it."

And so saying, he demanded of the thief, "Who are you?"

And she said, "Lord! I am a Yaksha."

And he asked, "Why did you take away this child?"

And she said, "I thought to eat him, O my Lord!"

And he rebuked her, saying, "O foolish woman! For your former sins you have been born a Yaksha, and do you still sin?" And he laid a vow upon her to keep the Five Commandments, and let her go.

But the mother of the child exalted the future Buddha, and said, "O my Lord! O great physician! May your life be long!" And she went away, with her babe clasped to her bosom.

5. THE MAN NAMED WISE

Once upon a time, the Bodhisattva was born in a merchant's family, and was given the name Wise. When he grew up he began doing business with a man whose name just happened to be Verywise.

It came to pass that Wise and Verywise took a caravan of 500 bullock carts into the countryside. After selling all their goods they returned to Benares with their handsome profits. When it came time to split their gains between them, Verywise said, "I should get twice as much profit as you."

"How come?" asked Wise.

"Because you are Wise and I am Verywise. It is obvious that Wise should get only half as much as Verywise."

Then Wise asked, "Didn't we both invest equal amounts in this caravan trip? Why do you deserve twice as much profit as I?"

Verywise replied, "Because of my quality of being Verywise."

In this way their quarrel went on with no end in sight.

Then Verywise thought, "I have a plan to win this argument." So he went to his father and asked him to hide inside a huge hollow tree. He said, "When my partner and I come by and ask how to share our profits, then you should say, 'Verywise deserves a double share.'"

Verywise returned to Wise and said, "My friend, neither of us wants this quarrel. Let's go to the old sacred tree and ask the tree spirit to settle it."

When they went to the tree, Verywise said solemnly, "My lord tree spirit, we have a problem. Kindly solve it for us."

Then his father, hidden inside the hollow tree, disguised his voice and asked, "What is your question?"

The man's cheating son said, "My lord tree spirit, this man is Wise and I am Verywise. We have done business together. Tell us how to share the profits."

Again disguising his voice, his father responded, "Wise deserves a single share and Verywise deserves a double share."

Hearing this solution, Wise decided to find out if it really was a tree spirit speaking from inside the tree. So he threw some hay into it and set it on fire. Immediately

Verywise's father grabbed onto a branch, jumped out of the flames and fell on the ground. He said in his own voice, "Although his name is Verywise, my son is just a clever cheater. I'm lucky that the one named Wise really is so and I've escaped only half toasted!"

Then Wise and Verywise shared their profits equally. Eventually they both died and were reborn as they deserved.

6. THE TWO MERCHANTS

Once upon a time, there were two merchants. They used to write letters back and forth to each other. They never met face to face. One lived in Benares and the other lived in a remote border village.

The country merchant sent a large caravan to Benares. It had 500 carts loaded with fruits, vegetables and other products. He told his workers to trade all these goods with the help of the Benares merchant.

When they arrived in the big city they went directly to the merchant. They gave him the gifts they had brought. He was pleased and invited them to stay in his own home. He even gave them money for their living expenses. He treated them with the very best hospitality. He asked about the well-being of the country merchant and gave them gifts to take back to him. Since it is easier for a local person to get a good price, he saw to it that all their goods were

fairly traded. They returned home and told their master all that had happened.

Later on, the Benares merchant sent a caravan of 500 carts to the border village. His workers also took gifts to the country merchant. When they arrived he asked:

"Where do you come from?" They said they came from the Benares merchant, the one who wrote him letters.

Taking the gifts, the country merchant laughed in a very discourteous way and said, "Anyone could say they came from the Benares merchant!" Then he sent them away, giving them no place to stay, no gifts, and no help at all. The caravan workers went downtown to the marketplace and did the best they could trading without local help. They returned to Benares and told their master all that had happened.

Before too long, the country merchant sent another caravan of 500 carts to Benares. Again his workers took gifts to the same merchant. When the Benares merchant's workers saw them coming, they said to him, "We know just how to provide suitable lodgings, food and expense money for these people."

They took them outside the city walls to a good place to camp for the night. They said they would return to Benares and prepare food and get expense money for them.

Instead they rounded up all their fellow workers and returned to the campsite in the middle of the night. They robbed all 500 carts, including the workers' outer garments. They chased away the bullocks, and removed and carried off the cart wheels.

The villagers were terrified. They ran back home as fast as their legs could carry them.

The city merchant's workers told him all they had done. He said, "Those who forget gratitude and ignore simple hospitality wind up getting what they deserve. Those who do not appreciate the help they have received, soon find that no one will help them anymore."

7. THE MASTER'S LAST WORDS

Once upon a time, the Bodhisattva was born into a high class family, and when he grew up, he became a holy man. Then he went to the Himalayan mountains where 500 other holy men became his followers.

He meditated throughout his long life. He gained supernatural powers - like flying through the air and understanding people's thoughts without their speaking. These special powers impressed his 500 followers greatly.

One rainy season, the chief follower took 250 of the holy men into the hill country villages to collect salt and other necessities. It just so happened that this was the time when the master (Bodhisattva) was about to die. The 250 who were still by his side realized this. So they asked him, "O most holy one, in your long life practising goodness and meditation, what was your greatest achievement?"

Having difficulty in speaking, as he was dying, the last words of the Bodhisattva were, "No Thing." Then he was reborn in a heaven world.

Expecting to hear about some fantastic magical power, the 250 followers were disappointed. They said to each other, "After a long life practising goodness and meditation our poor master has achieved 'nothing'." Since they considered him a failure, they burned his body with no special ceremony, honours, or even respect.

When the chief follower returned he asked, "Where is the holy one?"

"He has died," they told him. "Did you ask him about his greatest achievement?"

"Of course we did," they answered.

"And what did he say?" asked the chief follower.

"He said he achieved 'nothing'," they replied, "so we didn't celebrate his funeral with any special honours."

Then the chief follower said, "You brothers did not understand the meaning of the teacher's words. He achieved the great knowledge of 'No Thing'. He realized that the names of things are not what they are. There is what there is, without being called 'this thing' or 'that thing'. There is no 'Thing'."

In this way the chief follower explained the wonderful achievement of their great master, but they still did not understand.

Meanwhile, from his heaven world, the reborn Bodhisattva saw that his former chief follower's words were not accepted. So he left the heaven world and appeared floating in the air above his former followers' monastery. In praise of the chief follower's wisdom he said, "The one who hears the Truth and understands automatically, is far better off than a hundred fools who spend a hundred years thinking and thinking and thinking."

By preaching in this way, the Great Being encouraged the 500 holy men to continue seeking Truth. After lives spent in serious meditation, all 500 died and were reborn in the same heaven world with their former master.

8. THE CARPENTER AND HIS FOOLISH SON

Once upon a time, there dwelt a bald gray-haired carpenter in a village. One day, when he was planing away at some wood with his head glistening like a copper bowl, a mosquito settled on his scalp and stung him with its dart like sting.

Said the carpenter to his son, who was seated nearby, "My boy, there's a mosquito stinging me on the head. Do drive it away."

"Hold still then father," said the son. "One blow will settle it."

At that very time the Bodhisattva had reached that village in the way of trade, and was sitting in the carpenter's shop.

"Rid me of it!" cried the father.

"All right, father," answered the son, who was behind the old man's back, and, raising a sharp axe on high with intent to kill only the mosquito, he cleft his father's head into two. So the old man fell dead on the spot.

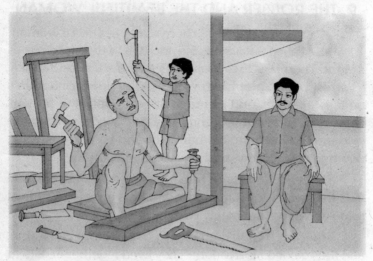

Thought the Bodhisattva, who had been an eye witness of the whole scene, "Better than such a friend is an enemy with sense, whom fear of men's vengeance will deter from killing a man." And he recited these lines:

"Sense-lacking friends are worse than foes with sense. Witness the son that sought the gnat to slay. But cleft, poor fool, his father's skull in two."

So saying, the Bodhisattva rose up and departed. And as for the carpenter, his body was burned by his kinsfolk.

9. THE ROBBER AND THE BEAUTIFUL WOMAN

Once upon a time, there was a beautiful woman, called Sulasa, whose price was a thousand pieces a night. There was in the same city a robber named Sattuka, as strong as an elephant, who used to enter rich men's houses at night and plunder at will. One day he was captured. Sulasa was standing at her window when the soldiers led Sattuka, his hands bound behind his back, down the street toward the place of execution.

She fell in love with him on sight, and said, "If I can free that stout fighting man, I will give up this bad life of mine and live respectably with him."

She sent a thousand pieces to the chief constable, and thus gained his freedom. They lived together in delight and harmony for some time, but after three or four months, the robber thought, "I shall never be able to stay in this one place. But one can't go empty handed. Her ornaments are worth a hundred thousand pieces. I will kill her and take them."

So he said to her one day, "Dear, when I was being hauled along by the King's men, I promised an offering to a tree deity on a mountain top, who is now threatening me because I have not paid it. Let us make an offering."

She consented to accompany her husband to the mountain top to make the offering. She should, he said, to honour the deity, wear all of her ornaments.

When they arrived at the mountain top, he revealed his true purpose, "I have not come to present the offering.

I have come with the intention of killing you and going away with all your ornaments. Take them all off and make a bundle of them in your outer garment."

"Husband, why would you kill me?"

"For your money."

"Husband, remember the good I have done you. When you were being hauled along in chains, I paid a large sum and saved your life. Though I might get a thousand pieces a day, I never look at another man. Such a benefactress I am to you. Do not kill me. I will give you much money and be your slave."

But instead of accepting her entreaties, he continued his preparations to kill her.

"At least let me salute you," she said. "I am going to make obeisance to you on all four sides." Kneeling in front

of him, she put her head to his foot, repeated the act at his left side, then at his right side, then from behind. Once behind him, she took hold of him, and with the strength of an elephant threw him over a cliff a hundred times as high as a man. He was crushed to pieces and died on the spot. Seeing this deed, the deity who lived on the mountain top spoke this stanza:

"Wisdom at times is not confined to men. A woman can show wisdom now and then."

So, Sulasa killed the robber. When she descended from the mountain and returned to her attendants, they asked where her husband was. "Don't ask me," she said, and mounting her chariot she went on to the city.

10. THE TWO GAMBLERS

Long, long ago, there was a rich man who was addicted to gambling. He played dice with another gambling addict, a man whose mind worked in tricky ways.

While the rich gambler was very honest and above board, the tricky one was dishonest. When he kept on winning he kept on playing. But when he began to lose he secretly put one of the dice in his mouth and swallowed it. Then he claimed it was lost and stopped the game.

The rich gambler began to notice this trick. One day he decided to teach him a lesson. He smeared poison on the dice and let it dry so it was invisible. He took these dice to the usual place and said, "Let's play dice!"

His friend agreed. They set up the gambling board and began to play. As usual the tricky one began by winning every throw of the dice. But as soon as he began to lose he sneaked the dice into his mouth.

Seeing this the rich gambler said, "Swallow now, and then something you don't expect will happen. Your own dishonesty will make you suffer much."

After swallowing the poison dice the trickster fell down sick and fainted. The rich gambler, who was basically good at heart, thought, "Enough is enough. Now I must save his life."

He made a medical mixture to cause vomiting. He made his friend swallow it, and he threw up the poison dice. He gave him a drink made with clear butter, thick palm syrup, honey and cane sugar. This made the trickster feel just fine again.

Afterwards he advised him not to deceive a trusting friend again. Eventually both gamblers died and were reborn as they deserved.

11. THE BRAVE PRINCE

Long, long ago, the son of Brahmadatta was ruling righteously in Benares. One day, the King of Kosala made war, killed the King of Benares, and made the Queen become his own wife.

Meanwhile, the Queen's son escaped by sneaking away through the sewers. In the countryside he eventually raised a large army and surrounded the city. He sent a message to the King, the murderer of his father and the husband of his mother. He told him to surrender the Kingdom or fight a battle.

The prince's mother, the Queen of Benares, heard of this threat from her son. She was a gentle and kind woman who wanted to prevent violence and suffering and killing. So she sent a message to her son – "There is no need for the risks of battle. It would be wiser to close every entrance to the city. Eventually the lack of food, water and firewood will wear down the citizens. Then they will give the city to you without any fighting."

The prince decided to follow his mother's wise advice. His army blockaded the city for seven days and nights.

Then the citizens captured their unlawful King, cut off his head, and delivered it to the prince. He entered the city triumphantly and became the new King of Benares.

12. THE KINDLY GOLDEN MALLARD

Once upon a time, the Bodhisattva was born as a Brahmin, and was married to a bride of his own rank, who bore him three daughters named Nanda, Nanda-vati, and Sundari-nanda. When the Bodhisattva died, they were taken in by neighbours and friends, whilst he was born again into the world as a golden mallard endowed with consciousness of its former existences.

Growing up, the bird viewed its own magnificent size and golden plumage, and remembered that previously it had been a human being. Discovering that his wife and daughters were living on the charity of others, the mallard bethought himself of his plumage like hammered and beaten gold and how by giving them a golden feather at a time he could enable his wife and daughters to live in comfort. So away he flew to where they dwelt and alighted on the top of the central beam of the roof. Seeing the Bodhisattva, the wife and girls asked where he had come from; and he told them that he was their father who had died and been born as a golden mallard, and that he had come to visit them and put an end to their miserable necessity of working for hire.

"You shall have my feathers," said he, "one by one, and they will sell for enough to keep you all in ease and comfort."

So saying, he gave them one of his feathers and departed. And from time to time he returned to give them another feather, and with the proceeds of their sale these Brahmin women grew prosperous and quite well to do.

But one day the mother said to her daughters, "There's no trusting animals, my children. Who's to say your father might not go away one of these days and never come back again? Let us use our time and pluck him clean next time he comes, so as to make sure of all his feathers."

Thinking this would pain him, the daughters refused.

The mother in her greed called the golden mallard to her one day when he came, and then took him with both hands and plucked him.

Now the Bodhisattva's feathers had this property that if they were plucked out against his wish, they ceased to be golden and became like a crane's feathers. And now the poor bird, though he stretched his wings, could not fly, and the woman flung him into a barrel and gave him food there. As time went on his feathers grew again though they were plain white ones now, and he flew away to his own abode and never came back again.

13. THE FOOLISH TORTOISE

Once upon a time, the Bodhisattva was born in a village as a potter's son. He plied the potter's trade, and had a wife and family to support.

At that time there lay a great natural lake close by the great river of Benares. When there was much water, river and lake were one; but when the water was low, they were apart. Now fish and tortoises know by instinct when the year will be rainy and when there will be a drought.

One day the fish and the tortoises which lived in that lake knew there would be a drought; and when the two were one water, they swam out of the lake into the river. But there was one tortoise that would not go into the river, because, said he, "Here I was born, and here I have grown up, and here is my parents' home. I cannot leave it!"

Then in the hot season the water all dried up. He dug a hole and buried himself, just in the place where the Bodhisattva was used to come for clay. There the Bodhisattva came to get some clay. With a big spade he dug down, until he cracked the tortoise's shell, turning him out on the ground as though he were a large piece of clay. In his agony the creature thought, "Here I am dying, all because I was too fond of my home to leave it!" And in the words of these following verses, he made his moan:

"Here was I born, and here I lived; My refuge was the clay; And now the clay has played me false in a most grievous way; Hear all of you what I have to say!

Go where you can find happiness, where'er the place may be; Forest or village, there the wise both home and birthplace see; Go where there's life; nor stay at home for death to master thee."

So he went on and on, talking to the Bodhisattva, until he died. The Bodhisattva picked him up, and collecting all the villagers addressed them thus:

"Look at this tortoise. When the other fish and tortoises went into the great river, he was too fond of home to go with them, and buried himself in the place where I get my clay. Then as I was digging for clay, I broke his shell with my big spade, and turned him out on the ground in the belief that he was a large lump of clay. Then he called to mind what he had done, lamented his fate in two verses of poetry, and expired. So you see he came to his end because he was too fond of his home. Take care not to be like this tortoise. Don't say to yourselves, 'I have sight, I have hearing, I have smell, I have taste, I have touch, I have a son, I have a daughter, I have numbers of men and maids for my service, I have precious gold.' Do not cleave to these things with craving and desire. Each being passes through three stages of existence."

Thus did he exhort the crowd with all a Buddha's skill. The discourse was bruited abroad all over India, and for full seven thousand years it was remembered. All the crowd abode by his exhortation, and gave alms, and did good until at last they went to swell the hosts of heaven.

14. THE KIND KING DEER

Once upon a time, there lived a beautiful golden deer in a forest. He was called King Banyan Deer and was the leader of a herd of five hundred deer. Not very far off, in the same forest was King Branch Deer who was also the leader amongst another five hundred deer. He was also extremely beautiful with a coat of a shiny golden hue and sparkling eyes.

Outside this beautiful forest, in the real world, there reigned a King who loved to eat meat at every single meal. He was King Brahmadatta of Benares. Not only was he fond of hunting, but he also enforced the same on his subjects. He forced them to leave their own businesses and join him regularly on his hunting spree each and every morning.

After a while the villagers got sick of this regular routine as they had much better things to do with their lives. Besides, their work and means of livelihood had also begun to suffer. They realised that they must find a solution. Together they came up with a plan.

They decided to grow plants, sow crops and dig water holes in the royal park itself. Then they would drive a number of deer into the confines of the park and shut the gates. In this way the King could hunt at leisure and would not require any further help from his obedient subjects.

So at first they went about preparing the royal park for the deer. Then they went into the forest armed with weapons and sticks in order to drive the deer into the royal park. They surrounded the territories of both the herds, those of King Banyan Deer as well as King Branch Deer, and drove them into the royal park, with shouts of glee as they beat their sticks on the ground and waved them in the air. As soon as both the herds were in, the gates were shut and the deer entrapped.

They then went to their King and told him that as they could not accompany him any more on his hunts they had successfully managed to entrap a number of deer in the royal park for his royal pleasure. The King was absolutely thrilled when he set eyes on the great number of deer in the royal park.

While gazing at them his eyes fell on the two beautiful golden deer and he at once decided to spare their lives. He issued an order that they were not to be shot at any cost. Each day after that, either the King or one of his hunters would shoot arrows at the deer. The deer would scatter wildly in every direction and get hurt in the ensuing stampede. So one day King Banyan Deer and King Branch

Deer put their heads together and came up with a plan. They realised that each day their herds were getting wounded in great numbers and some were getting killed. Even though death was inevitable they could at least try to save the living ones from unnecessary pain and torture.

So they decided to send a deer to the royal palace to be slaughtered and served to the King each and every day. The pact was to alternate between the two herds. In this way at least the rest of the deer would be spared unnecessary torture. This system continued for some time. Each day a deer was sent to the royal palace to be slaughtered by the royal cook. And the rest of the deer were allowed to live in peace until it was their turn.

One day it was the turn of a young female deer with a newborn baby. She belonged to the herd of King Branch Deer. She was worried that after she was killed there would be no one to take care of her child who was still too young to look after itself. So she approached her King with the plea that he send another deer instead of her that day and she would willingly go to the slaughter after her fawn was old enough to look after himself.

But King Branch Deer would not listen to her plea and told her to accept this as her fate as he could not ask another deer to replace her on the execution block. The mother doe looked at her baby and just could not take a step towards the palace. So she approached King Banyan Deer with her plea. King Banyan Deer looked at her with great compassion and told her to go look after her baby, as he would send another in her place.

Then King Banyan Deer himself walked to the palace and placed his head on the execution block. The royal cook was shocked to see him and remembering the King's orders, went running to the King to ask him what was to be done. The King came down to see what was happening.

On seeing King Banyan Deer he went up to him and gently asked why he was here. King Banyan Deer related the story of the fawn and the mother doe and told him that as he could not order another to take her place, he had decided to do it himself.

The King was highly impressed with this supreme sacrifice and the great love and compassion that this King of deer possessed. So he decided to not only spare his life but that of the mother doe as well.

But King Banyan Deer was not satisfied. He asked that the lives of the other deer be spared as well. So the King granted him his wish. Then he asked about all the other four-footed animals in the forest and then about the birds in the sky and the fish in the sea. And King Brahmadatta agreed to spare the lives of all. King Banyan Deer thanked him from the bottom of his heart and returned joyfully to the park. The gates were opened wide and both the herds were set free. Needless to say they lived peacefully and happily ever after.

15. THE STUPID LION

Once upon a time, there was a very wealthy man living in Benares who owned a large herd of cattle. He hired a man to look after them.

During the time of year when the rice paddies were filled with the green growing rice plants, the herdsman took the cattle to the forest to graze. From there he brought the milk and butter and cheese to the rich man in Benares.

It just so happened that being in the forest put the cattle in a very frightening situation. There was a meat eating lion living nearby. Sensing the presence of the lion kept the cattle in constant fear. This made the cows tense and high-strung, leaving them too weak to give more than a little milk.

One day the owner of the cattle asked the herdsman why he was bringing such a small amount of milk and

butter and cheese. He replied, "Sir, cows need to be calm and contented to give much milk. Due to a nearby lion, your cows are always afraid and tense. So they give hardly any milk."

"I see," said the rich man. Thinking like an animal trapper, he asked, "Is the lion closely connected to any other animal?"

The herdsman answered, "Sir, there happens to be a variety of deer living in the forest. They are called 'minideer' because they are so small. Even the adults only grow to be about one foot tall. The lion has become very friendly with a certain minideer doe."

The rich man of Benares said, "So that my cows will be at peace and able to give their usual milk, this is what you are to do. Capture the lion's friend and rub poison all over her body. Then wait a couple of days before releasing her. She will be like bait in a trap for the lion. When he dies, bring his body to me. Then my cows will be safe and happy again."

The herdsman followed his boss's orders exactly. When the lion saw his favourite minideer doe he was so overjoyed that he threw all caution to the wind. Without even sniffing the air around her, he immediately began licking her excitedly all over. Because of too much joy and not enough caution, he fell into the poisonous trap. The poor lion died on the spot.

16. THE TWO PARROTS

Once upon a time, the Bodhisattva was born as a young parrot. His name was Radha, and his youngest brother was named Potthapada. While they were yet quite young, both of them were caught by a fowler and handed over to a Brahmin in Benares. The Brahmin cared for them as if they were his children. But the Brahmin's wife was a wicked woman. There was no one to watch her.

The husband had to go away on business, and addressed his young parrots thus, "Little dears, I am going away on business. Keep watch on your mother in season and out of season. Observe whether or not any man visits her." So off he went, leaving his wife in charge of the young parrots.

As soon as he was gone, the woman began to do wrong. Night and day the visitors came and went. There was no end to them. Potthapada, observing this, said to Radha, "Our master gave this woman into our charge, and here she is doing wickedness. I will speak to her."

"Don't," said Radha.

But the other would not listen. "Mother," said he, "why do you commit sin?"

On hearing this, she longed to kill him! But making as though she would fondle him, she called him to her. "Little one, you are my son! I will never do it again! Come here then, my dear!"

So he came out. Then she seized him, crying, "What! You preach to me! You don't know your measure!" And she wrung his neck, and threw him into the oven.

The Brahmin returned. When he had rested, he asked the Bodhisattva, "Well, my dear, what about your mother? Does she do wrong or no?" And as he asked the question, he repeated the first couplet:

"I come, my son, the journey done, and now I am at home again. Come tell me, is your mother true? Does she betray me?"

Radha answered, "Father dear, the wise speak not of things which do not conduce to blessing, whether they have happened or not." And he explained this by repeating the second couplet:

"For what he said he now lies dead, burnt up beneath the ashes there. It is not well the truth to tell, lest Potthapada's fate I share."

Thus did the Bodhisattva hold forth to the Brahmin. And he went on, "This is no place for me to live in either." Then bidding the Brahmin farewell, he flew away into the woods.

17. THE HOLY MAN

Once upon a time, the Bodhisattva lived in a world where most religions were very similar. They taught that the way to remove suffering from the mind was to make the body suffer instead. As strange as it seems, most people thought that the holiest of the holy were the ones who tortured their bodies the most! Since everyone seemed to agree with this, the Bodhisattva decided to find out for himself if it was true.

He stopped living as an ordinary everyday person and became a holy man according to the custom of the times. This meant that he gave up everything, even his clothes. He went naked, with his body covered only by dust and dirt.

So he wouldn't be spoiled by the taste of good food, he forced himself to eat only filthy things – dirt, ashes, urine and cow dung.

Now he could concentrate without being interrupted by anyone, and he went to live in the most dangerous part of the forest. If he did see a human being, he ran away like a timid deer.

In the winter time he spent his days under the trees and his nights out in the open. So in the daytime he was soaked by the cold water dripping from the icicles hanging

from the tree branches. And at night he was covered by the falling snow. In this way, in winter, he made his body suffer the most extreme cold during both day and night.

In the summer time he spent his days out in the open and his nights under the trees. So in the daytime he was burned by the most severe rays of the sun. And at night he was blocked from the few cooling breezes of the open air. In this way, in summer, he made his body suffer the most extreme heat during both day and night.

This was how he struggled, trying to bring peace to his mind. He was so determined that he lived his entire life in this way.

Then, just as he was about to die, he saw a vision of himself reborn in a hell world. The vision struck him like lightning, and instantly he knew that all the ways he had tortured his body were completely useless! They had not brought him peace of mind. Lo and behold, as he gave up his false beliefs and held on to the truth, he died and was reborn in a heaven world!

18. THE CROCODILE AND THE MONKEY

Once upon a time, the Bodhisattva was born as a monkey at the foot of the Himalayas. He grew strong and sturdy, big of frame, well to do, and lived by a curve of the river Ganges in a forest haunt. Now at that time there was a crocodile dwelling in the Ganges. The crocodile's mate saw the great frame of the monkey, and she conceived a longing to eat his heart. So she said to her lord, "Sir, I desire to eat the heart of that great King of the monkeys!"

"Good wife," said the crocodile, "I live in the water and he lives on dry land. How can we catch him?"

"By hook or by crook," she replied, "he must be caught. If I don't get him, I shall die."

"All right," answered the crocodile, consoling her, "don't trouble yourself. I have a plan. I will give you his heart to eat."

So when the Bodhisattva was sitting on the bank of the Ganges, after taking a drink of water, the crocodile drew near, and said, "Sir Monkey, why do you live on bad fruits in this old familiar place? On the other side of the Ganges there is no end to the mango trees, and labuja trees, with fruits sweet as honey! Is it not better to cross over and have all kinds of wild fruit to eat?"

"Lord Crocodile," the monkey answered. "The Ganges is deep and wide. How shall I get across?"

"If you want to go, I will let you sit upon my back, and carry you over."

The monkey trusted him, and agreed. "Come here, then," said the crocodile. "Up on my back with you!" and up the monkey climbed.

But when the crocodile had swum a little way, he plunged the monkey under the water.

"Good friend, you are letting me sink!" cried the monkey. "What is that for?"

The crocodile said, "You think I am carrying you out of pure good nature? Not a bit of it! My wife has a longing for your heart, and I want to give it to her to eat!"

"Friend," said the monkey, "it is nice of you to tell me. Why, if our heart were inside us, when we go jumping among the tree tops it would be all knocked to pieces!"

"Well, where do you keep it?" asked the crocodile.

The Bodhisattva pointed out a fig tree, with clusters of ripe fruit, standing not far off. "See," said he, "there are our hearts hanging on yonder fig tree."

"If you will show me your heart," said the crocodile, "then I won't kill you."

"Take me to the tree, then, and I will point it out to you."

The crocodile brought him to the place. The monkey leapt off his back, and, climbing up the fig tree, sat upon it. "O silly crocodile!" said he. "You thought that there were creatures that kept their hearts in a treetop! You are a fool, and I have outwitted you! You may keep your fruit to yourself. Your body is great, but you have no sense."

And then to explain this idea he uttered the following stanzas:

"Rose-apple, jack-fruit, mangoes, too, across the water there I see; Enough of them, I want them not; my fig is good enough for me! Great is your body, verily, but how much smaller is your wit! Now go your ways, Sir Crocodile, for I have had the best of it."

The crocodile, feeling as sad and miserable as if he had lost a thousand pieces of money, went back sorrowing to the place where he lived.

19. THE KING OF THE WORLD

Once upon a time, the Bodhisattva was born and given the name 'Clear-sighted'. As he grew up he developed ten rules of good government: absence of hidden ill will, absence of open hostility, harmlessness, self-control, patience, gentleness, charity, generosity, straightforwardness and goodness.

The people of the world began to notice the wholesomeness and fairness of Clear-sighted, who lived strictly according to these rules. Gradually those in his vicinity volunteered to live under his authority as King, rather than under the dishonest politicians of the time.

As his reputation spread, every King in the world came to Clear-sighted and said, "Come, O lord. You are welcome. My Kingdom is your Kingdom. Advise me how to rule in your name."

Then Clear-sighted said, "Do not destroy life. Do not take what is not given. Do not behave wrongly in sexual desires. Do not speak falsely. Do not take alcohol that clouds the mind. My commands to the world are only these five. As long as these five are obeyed, my sixth rule is freedom for all to follow local customs and religions."

After all the people on earth had come to live under his peaceful rule, he became known as Clear-sighted the Great, King of the World. His royal city, the capital of the whole world, was called Kusavati. It was a beautiful and prosperous city with four magnificent gates - one golden, one silver, one jade and one crystal.

Outside the gates, Kusavati was surrounded by seven rows of palm trees - a row with golden trunks and silver leaves and fruits; a row with silver trunks and golden leaves and fruits; a row with cat's-eye trunks and crystal leaves and fruits; a row with crystal trunks and cat's-eye leaves and fruits; a row with agate trunks and coral leaves and fruits; a row with coral trunks and agate leaves and fruits; and finally a row with trunks and leaves and fruits of every kind of jewel found in the world!

When breezes blew through these marvelous palms the sweet sounds of gentle music were heard throughout the city. This music was so enticing and pleasant that some of the citizens were enchanted into stopping their work and dancing for joy!

Clear-sighted the Great, King of the World, had a couch encrusted with jewels from the wonderful palms. After a long, righteous and peaceful reign, he lay on the rich couch for the last time. He knew that his end was near. Of all his 84,000 Queens, the one who loved him most was called, 'Most-pleasant'. Sensing the state of his mind she said, "You rule over all the cities of the world, including this beautiful Kusavati with its four magnificent gates and seven rows of marvelous palms. Think about this and be happy!"

The King of the World said, "No, my dear Queen, don't say that. Instead you should advise me to give up attachment to the cities of the world and all they contain."

Surprised, she asked, "Why do you say this, my lord?"

"Because today I will die," he said.

Then Queen Most-pleasant started to cry, wiping away the tears as they flowed. And all the other Queens also broke into tears. And the King's ministers and his whole court, both men and women, could not keep from weeping and sobbing. All eyes overflowed with tears.

But King Clear-sighted the Great said, "Your tears are useless. Be at peace." Hearing this the wailing subsided and his subjects became silent. Then he said to Queen Most-pleasant, "O my Queen, do not cry, do not lament. Anything that comes into being, whether it be a Kingdom including the whole world, or just a tiny sesame seed – it cannot last forever. Anyone who comes into being, whether it be the King of the World, or the poorest petty thief – all must die and decay. Whatever is built up, falls apart. Whatever becomes, decays. The only true happiness is in the moment when becoming and decaying are not."

In this way the Bodhisattva got them to think about what most people don't want to think about – that all things come to an end. He advised them to be generous and wholesome. Then the King of the World, like everyone else, died. He was reborn as a god in a heaven world, where in time, like everyone else, he died.

20. THE MAN NAMED BAD

Once upon a time, there was a world famous teacher. He had 500 students who learned sacred teachings from him.

It just so happened that one of these students had been named 'Bad' by his parents. One day he thought, "When I am told, 'Come Bad', 'Go Bad', 'Do this Bad', it is not nice for me or others. It even sounds disgraceful and unlucky."

So he went to the teacher and asked him to give him a more pleasant name, one that would bring good fortune rather than bad.

The teacher said, "Go my son, go wherever you like and find a more fortunate name. When you return, I will officially give you your new name."

The young man named Bad left the city, and travelled from village to village until he came to a big city. A man had just died and Bad asked what his name was.

People said. "His name was Alive."

"Alive also died?" asked Bad.

The people answered, "Whether his name be Alive or whether it be Dead, in either case he must die. A name is merely a word used to recognize a person. Only a fool would not know this!"

After hearing this, Bad no longer felt badly about his own name - but he didn't feel good about it either.

As he continued on his way into the city, a debt-slave girl was being beaten by her masters in the street.

He asked, "Why is she being beaten?"

He was told, "Because she is a slave until she pays a loan debt to her masters. She has come home from working, with no wages to pay as interest on her debt."

"And what is her name?" he asked.

"Her name is Rich," they said.

"By her name she is Rich, but she has no money even to pay interest?" asked Bad.

They said, 'Whether her name be Rich or whether it be Poor, in either case she has no money. A name is merely a word used to recognize a person. Only a fool would not know this!"

After hearing this, Bad became even less interested in changing his name.

After leaving the city, along the roadside he met a man who had lost his way. He asked him, "What is your name?"

The man replied, "My name is Tourguide."

"You mean to say that even a Tourguide has gotten lost?" asked Bad.

Then the man said, "Whether my name be Tourguide or whether it be Tourist, in either case I have lost my way. A name is merely a word used to recognize a person. Only a fool would not know this!"

Now completely satisfied with his own name, Bad returned to his teacher.

The world famous teacher of Takshasila asked him, "How are you, my son? Have you found a good name?"

He answered, "Sir, those named Alive and Dead both die, Rich and Poor may be penniless, Tourguide and Tourist can get lost. Now I know that a name is merely a word used to recognize a person. The name does not make things happen, only deeds do. So I'm satisfied with my name. There's no point in changing it."

21. THE STUPID TORTOISE

Once upon a time, the Bodhisattva was born in a minister's family; and when he grew up, he became the King's adviser in things temporal and spiritual.

Now this King was very talkative; while he was speaking, others had no opportunity for a word. And the future Buddha, wanting to cure this talkativeness of his, was constantly seeking for some means of doing so.

At that time there was living, in a pond in the Himalayan Mountains, a tortoise. Two young wild ducks who came to feed there made friends with him. And one day, when they had become very intimate with him, they said to the tortoise, "Friend tortoise, the place where we live, at the Golden Cave on Mount Beautiful in the Himalayan country, is a delightful spot. Will you come there with us?"

"But how can I get there?"

"We can take you, if you can only hold your tongue, and will say nothing to anybody."

"Oh, that I can do. Take me with you."

"That's right," said they. And making the tortoise bite hold of a stick, they themselves took the two ends in their teeth, and flew up into the air.

Seeing him thus carried by the ducks, some villagers called out, "Two wild ducks are carrying a tortoise along on a stick!"

Whereupon the tortoise wanted to say, "If my friends choose to carry me, what is that to you, you wretched slaves?" So just as the swift flight of the wild ducks had brought him over the King's palace in the city of Benares, he let go of the stick he was biting, and falling in the open courtyard, split in two!

And there arose a universal cry, "A tortoise has fallen in the open courtyard, and has split in two!"

The King, taking the future Buddha, went to the place, surrounded by his courtiers, and looking at the tortoise, he asked the Bodhisattva, "Teacher, how was it possible that he has fallen here?"

The future Buddha thought to himself, "Long expecting, wishing to admonish the King, I have sought for some means of doing so. This tortoise must have made friends with the wild ducks; and they must have made him bite hold of the stick, and have flown up into the air to take him to the hills. But he, being unable to hold his tongue when he hears anyone else talk, must have wanted to say something, and let go of the stick; and so must have fallen down from the sky, and thus lost his life." And saying, "Truly, O King, those who are called chatterboxes – people whose words have no end – come to grief like this," he uttered these verses:

"Verily, the tortoise killed himself while uttering his voice. Though he was holding tight to stick, by a word he slew himself. Behold him then, O excellent by strength! And speak wise words, not out of season. You see how, by his talking overmuch, the tortoise fell into this wretched plight!"

The King saw that he was himself referred to, and said, "O teacher, are you speaking of us?"

And the Bodhisattva spoke openly, and said, "O great King, be it you, or be it any other, whoever talks beyond measure meets with some mishap like this."

And the King henceforth refrained himself, and became a man of few words.

22. THE JUDAS TREE

The King of Benares, Brahmadatta, had four sons. One day they sent for the charioteer and said to him, "We want to see a Judas tree. Show us one!"

"Very well, I will," the charioteer replied.

But he did not show it to them all together. He took the eldest at once to the forest in the chariot, and showed him the tree at the time when the buds were just sprouting from the stem. To the second he showed it when the leaves were green. To the third at the time of blossoming. And to the fourth when it was bearing fruit.

After this it happened that the four brothers were sitting together and someone asked, "What sort of a tree is the Judas tree?"

Then the first brother answered, "Like a burnt stump!"

And the second cried, "Like a banyan tree!"

And the third, "Like a piece of meat!"

And the fourth said, "Like the acacia!"

They were vexed at each other's answers, and ran to find their father.

"My Lord," they asked, "what sort of a tree is the Judas tree?"

"What did you say to that?" he asked.

They told him the manner of their answers.

Said the King, "All four of you have seen the tree. Only when the charioteer showed you the tree, you did not ask him, 'What is the tree like at such a time, or at such another time?' You made no distinctions, and that is the reason of your mistake."

And he repeated the first stanza:

"All have seen the Judas tree. What is your perplexity? No one asked the charioteer 'What its form the livelong year!'"

23. THE STUPID HARE

Once upon a time, the Bodhisattva came to life as a young lion, and when he fully grown he lived in a wood. At this time there was near the Western Ocean a grove of palms mixed with vilva trees.

A certain hare lived here beneath a palm sapling, at the foot of a vilva tree. One day this hare, after feeding, came and lay down beneath the young palm tree. And the thought struck him, "If this earth should be destroyed, what would become of me?"

And at this very moment a ripe vilva fruit fell on a palm leaf. At the sound of it, the hare thought, "This solid earth is collapsing," and starting up he fled, without so much as looking behind him. Another hare saw him scampering off, as if frightened to death, and asked the cause of his panic flight.

"Pray, don't ask me," he said.

The other hare cried, "Pray, sir, what is it?" and kept running after him.

Then the hare stopped a moment and without looking back said, "The earth here is breaking up."

And at this the second hare ran after the other. And so first one and then another hare caught sight of him running, and joined in the chase till one hundred thousand hares all took to flight together. They were seen by a deer, a boar, an elk, a buffalo, a wild ox, a rhinoceros, a tiger, a lion and an elephant. And when they asked what it meant and were told that the earth was breaking up, they too took to flight. So by degrees this host of animals extended to the length of a full league.

When the Bodhisattva saw this headlong flight of the animals, and heard the cause of it was that the earth was coming to an end, he thought, "The earth is nowhere coming to an end. Surely it must be some sound which was misunderstood by them. And if I don't make a great effort, they will all perish. I will save their lives."

So with the speed of a lion he got before them to the foot of a mountain, and roared three times. They were terribly frightened of the lion, and stopping in their flight stood all huddled together. The lion went in amongst them and asked why there were running away.

"The earth is collapsing," they answered.

"Who saw it collapsing?" he asked.

"The elephants know all about it," they replied.

He asked the elephants. "We don't know," they said, "the lions know."

But the lions said, "We don't know, the tigers know."

The tigers said, "The rhinoceroses know."

The rhinoceroses said, "The wild oxen know."

The wild oxen said, "The buffaloes."

The buffaloes said, "The elks."

The elks said, "The boars."

The boars said, "The deer."

The deer said, "We don't know, the hares know."

When the hares were questioned, they pointed to one particular hare and said, "This one told us."

So the Bodhisattva asked, "Is it true, sir, that the earth is breaking up?"

"Yes, sir, I saw it," said the hare.

"Where," he asked, "were you living, when you saw it?"

"Near the ocean, sir, in a grove of palms mixed with vilva trees. For as I was lying beneath the shade of a palm sapling at the foot of a vilva tree, methought, 'If this earth should break up, where shall I go?' And at that very moment I heard the sound, the breaking up of the earth, and I fled."

Thought the lion, "A ripe vilva fruit evidently must have fallen on a palm leaf and made a 'thud,' and this hare jumped to the conclusion that the earth was coming to an end, and ran away. I will find out the exact truth about it."

So he reassured the herd of animals, and said, "I will take the hare and go and find out exactly whether the earth is coming to an end or not, in the place pointed out by him. Until I return, you do stay here."

Then placing the hare on his back, he sprang forward with the speed of a lion, and putting the hare down in the palm grove, he said, "Come, show us the place you meant."

"I dare not, my lord," said the hare.

"Come, don't be afraid," said the lion.

The hare, not venturing to go near the vilva tree, stood afar off and cried, "Yonder, sir, is the place of dreadful sound," and so saying, he repeated the first stanza:

"From the spot where I did dwell issued forth a fearful thud'. What it was I could not tell, nor what caused it understood."

After hearing what the hare said, the lion went to the foot of the vilva tree, and saw the spot where the hare had been lying beneath the shade of the palm tree, and the ripe vilva fruit that fell on the palm leaf, and having carefully ascertained that the earth had not broken up, he placed the hare on his back and with the speed of a lion soon came again to the herd of beasts.

Then he told them the whole story, and said, "Don't be afraid." And having thus reassured the herd of beasts, he let them go.

Verily, if it had not been for the Bodhisattva at that time, all the beasts would have rushed into the sea and perished. It was all owing to the Bodhisattva that they escaped death.

24. THE FATHER AND HIS SEVEN-YEAR-OLD CHILD

Once upon a time, there was a rich man who had an intelligent and curious son. Even though he was only seven years old, he was determined to find out what is really valuable.

One day the little boy asked his father, "What are the ways to gain the most valuable things in life?"

His father said, "Only worthy ways lead to worthwhile goals. These are the six worthy ways:

- ♦ keep yourself healthy and fit;
- ♦ be wholesome in every way;
- ♦ listen to those with more experience;
- ♦ learn from those with more knowledge;
- ♦ live according to truth;
- ♦ act with sincerity, not just energy."

The boy paid close attention to his father's words. He tried hard to practise those ways from then on. As he grew up and became wise, he realized that the six worthy ways, and the most valuable things in life, could not be separated.

25. THE HERO NAMED JINX

Once upon a time, there was a very rich man who had a good friend, named Jinx. They had been the best of friends ever since they were little children making mud-pies together. They had gone to the same schools and helped each other always.

After graduating, Jinx fell on hard times. He couldn't find a job and earn a living. So he went to see his lifelong friend, the prosperous and successful rich man. He was kind and comforting to his friend Jinx, and was happy to hire him to manage his property and business.

After he went to work in the rich man's mansion pretty soon his strange name became a household word. People said, "Wait a minute, Jinx," "Hurry up, Jinx," "Do this, Jinx," "Do that, Jinx."

After a while some of the rich man's neighbours went to him and said, "Dear friend and neighbour, we are concerned that misfortune may strike. Your mansion manager has a very strange and unlucky name. You should not let him live with you any longer. His name fills your house, with people saying, "Wait a minute, Jinx," "Hurry up, Jinx," "Do this, Jinx," "Do that, Jinx." People only use the word 'Jinx' when they want to cause bad luck or misfortune. Even house spirits and fairies would be frightened by hearing it constantly and would run away. This can only bring disaster to your household. The man named Jinx is inferior to you - he is miserable and ugly. What advantage can you possibly get by keeping such a fellow around?"

The rich man replied, "Jinx is my best friend! We have supported and cared for each other ever since we were little tots making mud-pies together. A lifelong trustworthy friend is of great value indeed! I could not reject him and lose our friendship just because of his name. After all, a name is only for recognition.

"The wise don't give a name a second thought. Only fools are superstitious about sounds and words and names. They don't make good luck or bad luck!" So saying, the rich man refused to follow the advice of his busybody neighbours.

One day he went on a journey to his home village. While he was away, he left his friend Jinx in charge of his mansion home.

It just so happened that a gang of robbers heard about this. They decided it would be a perfect time to rob the mansion. So they armed themselves with various weapons and surrounded the rich man's home during the night.

Meanwhile, the faithful Jinx suspected that robbers might attack. So he stayed up all night to guard his friend's possessions. When he caught sight of the gang surrounding the house, he woke up everybody inside. Then he got them to blow shell horns and beat drums and make as much noise as possible.

Hearing all this, the bandits thought, "We must have been given wrong information. There must be many people inside and the rich man must still be at home." So they threw down their clubs and other weapons, and ran away.

The next morning the people from the mansion were surprised to see the discarded weapons. They said to each other, "If we didn't have such a wise house protector, all the wealth in the mansion would certainly have been stolen. Jinx has turned out to be a hero! Rather than bringing bad luck, such a strong friend has been a blessing to the rich man."

When the master of the house returned home his neighbours met him and told him what had happened. He said, "You all advised against letting my friend stay with me. If I had done as you said, I'd be penniless today!

"Walking together for just seven steps is enough to start a friendship. Continuing for twelve steps forms a bond of loyalty. Remaining together for a month brings the closeness of relatives. And for longer still, the friend becomes like a second self. So my friend Jinx is no jinx - but a great blessing!"

26. THE GREAT KING

Once upon a time, the Bodhisattva was born into the royal family, and when he became King he was called Goodness the Great. He had earned this title by trying to do good all the time, even when the results might not benefit him. For example, he spent much of the royal treasury on the building and running of six houses for charity. In these houses food and aid were given freely to all the poor and needy, even to unknown travellers who came along. Soon King Goodness the Great became famous for his patience, loving-kindness and compassion. It was said that he loved all beings just like a father loves his young children.

Of course King Goodness observed the holy days by not eating. And naturally he practised the 'Five Training Steps', giving up the five unwholesome actions. These are: destroying life, taking what is not given, doing wrong in sexual ways, speaking falsely, and losing one's mind with alcohol. So his gentle kindness became more and more pure.

Since he wished to harm no one, King Goodness the Great even refused to imprison or injure wrongdoers. Knowing this, one of his highest ministers tried to take advantage of him. He cooked up a scheme to cheat some of the women in the royal harem. Afterwards it became known by all and was reported to the King.

He called the bad minister before him and said, "I have investigated and found that you have done a criminal act. Word of it has spread that you have dishonoured yourself here in Benares. So it would be better for you to go and live somewhere else. You may take all your wealth and your family. Go wherever you like and live happily there. Learn from this lesson."

Then the minister took his family and all his belongings to the city of Kosala. Since he was very clever indeed, he worked his way up and became a minister of the King. In time he became the most trusted adviser to the King of Kosala.

One day he said, "My lord, I came here from Benares. The city of Benares is like a beehive where the bees have no stings! The ruling King is very tender and weak. With only a very small army you can easily conquer the city and make it yours."

The King doubted this, so he said, "You are my minister, but you talk like a spy who is leading me into a trap!"

He replied, "No, my lord. If you don't believe me, send your best spies to examine what I say. I am not lying. When robbers are brought to the King of Benares, he gives

them money, advises them not to take what is not given, and then lets them go free."

The King decided to find out if this was true. So he sent some robbers to raid a remote border village belonging to Benares. The villagers caught the looters and brought them to King Goodness the Great. He asked them, "Why do you want to do this type of crime?"

The robbers answered, "Your Worship, we are poor people. There is no way to live without money. As your Kingdom has plenty of workers, there is no work for us to do. So we had to loot the country in order to survive." Hearing this, the King gave them gifts of money, advised them to change their ways, and let them go free.

When the King of Kosala was told of this, he sent another gang of bandits to the streets of Benares itself.

They too looted the shops and even killed some of the people. When they were captured and brought to King Goodness, he treated them just the same as the first robbers.

Learning of this, the King of Kosala began marching his troops and elephants towards Benares.

In those days the King of Benares had a mighty army which included very brave elephants. There were many ordinary soldiers, and also some who were as big as giants. It was known that they were capable of conquering all India.

The giant soldiers told King Goodness about the small invading army from Kosala. They asked permission to attack and kill them all.

But King Goodness the Great would not send them into battle. He said, "My children, do not fight with them. If we destroy the lives of others, we also destroy our own peace of mind. Why should we kill others? Let them have the Kingdom if they want it so badly. I do not wish to fight."

The royal ministers said, "Our lord, we will fight them ourselves. Don't worry yourself. Only give us the order." But again he prevented them.

Meanwhile the King of Kosala sent him a warning, telling him to give up the Kingdom or fight. King Goodness the Great sent this reply, "I do not want you to fight with me, and you do not want me to fight with you. If you want the country, you can have it. Why should we kill people just to decide the name of the King? What does it matter even the name of the country itself?"

Hearing this, the ministers came forward and pleaded, "Our lord, let us go out with our mighty army. We will beat them with our weapons and capture them all. We are much stronger than they. We would not have to kill any of them. And besides, if we surrender the city, the enemy army would surely kill us all!"

But King Goodness would not be moved. He refused to cause harm to anyone. He replied, "Even if you do not wish to kill, by fighting many will be injured. By accident some may die. No one knows the future – whether our present actions are right or wrong. Therefore I will not harm, or cause others to harm, any living being!"

Then King Goodness ordered the city gates be opened up for the invaders. He took his ministers to the top floor of the palace and advised them, "Say nothing and try to remain calm."

The King of Kosala entered the city of Benares and saw that no one was against him. He surrounded the royal palace. He found that even the palace doors were open to him. So he and his soldiers entered and went up to the top floor. They captured the innocent King Goodness the Great. The soldiers tied the hands of the defeated King and all his ministers.

Then they were taken to the cemetery outside the city. They were buried up to their necks, standing straight up, with only their heads above ground. But even while the dirt was being trampled down around his neck, the Great Being remained without anger in his mind and said nothing.

Their discipline and obedience to King Goodness were so great that not a single minister spoke a word against anyone. But the King of Kosala had no mercy. He said roughly, "Come nighttime, let the jackals do as they please!"

And so it came to pass that, at midnight, a large band of jackals wandered into the cemetery. They could smell a feast of human flesh waiting for them.

Seeing them coming, King Goodness and his ministers shouted all at once and scared the jackals away. Twice more this happened. Then the clever jackals realised, "These men must have been put here for us to kill and eat." No longer afraid, they ignored the shouts. The jackal King walked right up to the face of King Goodness.

The King offered his throat to the beast. But before he could bite into him, the King grabbed the jackal's chin with his teeth. Not harming him, King Goodness gripped him tightly so that the jackal King howled in fear. This frightened his followers and they all ran away.

Meanwhile the jackal King thrashed back and forth, trying madly to free himself from the mighty jaws of the human King. In so doing, he loosened the dirt packed around the King's neck and shoulders. Then King Goodness released the screaming jackal. He was able to wriggle himself free from the loosened earth and pull himself up onto the ground. Then he freed all his frightened ministers.

Nearby there was a dead body. It just so happened that it was lying on the border of the territories claimed by two rival demons. They were arguing over the division of the body, insulting each other in ways that only demons can.

Then one demon said to the other, "Why should we continue quarrelling instead of eating? Right over there is King Goodness the Great of Benares. He is famous in all worlds for his righteousness. He will divide the dead body for us."

They dragged the body to the King and asked him to divide it between them fairly. He said, "My dear friends, I would be glad to divide this for you. But I am filthy and dirty. I must clean myself first."

The two demons used their magic powers to bring scented water, perfume, clothing, ornaments and flowers from the King's own palace in Benares. He bathed, perfumed himself, dressed, and covered himself with ornaments and flower garlands.

The demons asked King Goodness if there was anything else they could do. He replied that he was hungry. So, again by their magic powers, the demons brought the most delicious flavoured rice in a golden bowl and perfumed drinking water in a golden cup - also from the royal palace in Benares.

When he was satisfied, King Goodness asked them to bring him the sword of state from the pillow of the King of Kosala, who was sleeping in the palace in Benares. With magic this too was easily done. Then the King used the sword to cut the dead body in two halves, right down the spine. He washed the sword of state and strapped it to his side.

The hungry demons happily gobbled up the fairly divided dead body. Then they gratefully said to King Goodness, "Now that our bellies are full, is there anything else we can do to please you?"

He replied, "By your magic, set me in my own bedroom in the palace next to the King of Kosala. In addition, put all my ministers back in their homes." Without a word, the demons did exactly as the King had asked.

At that moment the King of Kosala was fast asleep in the royal bed chamber. King Goodness the Great gently touched the belly of the sleeping King with the sword of state. The King awoke in great surprise. In the dim lamplight he was frightened to see King Goodness leaning over him with sword in hand. He had to rub his eyes to make sure he was not having a nightmare!

Then he asked the great King, "My lord, how did you come here in spite of all my guards? You were buried up to your neck in the cemetery – how is it you are spotlessly clean, sweet smelling, dressed in your own royal robes, and decorated with fine jewellery and the loveliest flowers?"

King Goodness told him the story of his escape from the band of jackals. He told of the two demons who came to him to settle their quarrel. And he told how they gratefully helped him with their magic powers.

On hearing this, the King of Kosala was overcome by his own shame. He bowed his head to King Goodness the Great and cried, "O great King, the stupid ferocious demons, who live by eating the flesh and drinking the blood of dead bodies – they recognised your supreme goodness. But I, who was lucky enough to be born as an intelligent and civilised human being, have been too foolish to see how wonderful your pure goodness is."

"I promise never again to plot against you, my lord – you who have gained such perfect harmlessness. And I promise to serve you forever as the truest of friends. Please forgive me, great King." Then, as if he were a servant, the King of Kosala laid King Goodness the Great down on the royal bed, while he himself lay on a small couch.

The next day the King of Kosala called all his soldiers into the palace courtyard. There he publicly praised the King of Benares and asked his forgiveness once again. He gave back the Kingdom and promised that he would always protect King Goodness. Then he punished his adviser, the criminal minister, and returned to Kosala with all his troops and elephants.

King Goodness the Great was sitting majestically on his golden throne, with its legs like those of a gazelle. He was shaded from the sun by the pure white royal umbrella. He taught his loyal subjects saying, "People of Benares, wholesomeness begins with giving up the five unwholesome actions once and for all. The highest qualities of the good person, whether ruler or subject, are loving-kindness and compassion. Filled with these qualities, one cannot harm another – no matter what the reason or the cost. No matter how dangerous the threat, one must persevere until the greatness of the good heart wins in the end."

Throughout the rest of his reign, the people of Benares lived peacefully and happily. King Goodness the Great continued performing wholesome works. Eventually he died and was reborn as he deserved.

🐘 🐘 🐘

27. THE KING AND THE ROYAL PRIEST

Once upon a time, there was a King who loved to gamble with his royal priest. When he threw the dice, he always recited this lucky charm:

"If tempted, any woman will, for sure, give up her faithfulness and act impure."

Amazing as it may seem, by using this charm the King always won! Before long, the royal priest lost almost every penny he owned.

He thought, "I have lost almost all my wealth to the King. It must be because of his lucky charm. I need to find a way to break the spell and win back my money. I must find a pure woman who has never had anything to do with a man. Then I will lock her up in my mansion and force her to remain faithful to me!"

This seemed like a good plan to him. But then he started having doubts. He thought, "It would be nearly impossible to keep a woman pure after she has already become accustomed to men. Therefore I must find the purest woman possible – one who has never even seen a man!"

Just then he happened to see a poor woman passing by. She was pregnant. The royal priest was an expert in reading the meaning of marks on the body. So he could tell that the unborn baby was a girl. And the thought occurred to him, "Aha! Only an unborn baby girl has never seen a man!"

The royal priest was willing to do anything to beat the King at dice. So he paid the poor woman to stay in his house and have her baby there. When the wonderful little girl was born, the priest bought her from her mother. Then he made sure she was raised only by women. She never saw a man - except of course the royal priest himself. When she grew up, he still kept her completely under his control. It was just as if he owned the poor girl!

The cruel priest did all this only because of his gambling habit. While the girl was growing up, he had avoided playing dice with the King. Now that she was of age, and still his prisoner, he challenged the King to a game of dice once again.

The King agreed. After they had made their bets, the King shook the dice and repeated his favourite lucky charm:

"If tempted, any woman will, for sure, give up her faithfulness and act impure."

But just before he threw down the dice, the priest added:

"Except my woman – faithful evermore!"

Lo and behold, the King's charm didn't work. He lost that bet, and from then on the priest won every throw of the dice.

The King was puzzled by this turn of events. After considering, he thought, "This priest must have a pure woman locked up at home, one who is forced to be faithful to him alone. That's why my lucky charm doesn't work anymore."

He investigated and discovered what the cruel priest had done. So he sent for a well-known playboy character. He asked him if he could cause the lady's downfall. He replied, "No problem, my lord!" The King paid him handsomely and told him to do the job quickly.

The man bought a supply of the finest perfumes and cosmetics. He set up a shop just outside the royal priest's mansion. This mansion was seven storeys high, with seven entrance gates – one on each floor. Each gate was guarded by women, and no man except the priest was allowed to enter.

The priest's lady was waited on by only one servant. She carried everything in and out, including perfumes and cosmetics. The priest gave her money for her purchases.

The playboy saw the servant going in and out of the priest's mansion. Soon he realised she was the one who could get him inside. So he devised a plan and hired some cronies to help him.

The next morning, when the serving lady went out to do her shopping, the playboy dramatically fell to the ground before her. Grabbing her knees tearfully cried, "O my dear mother, it's so wonderful to see you again after such a long time!"

Then his cronies chimed in, "Yes, yes, this must be she! She looks the same – her hands and feet and face and type of dress. Yes, yes, this must be she!" They all kept saying how amazing it was that her looks had changed so little in all that time.

The poor woman must have had a long lost son, for soon she was convinced this must be he. She hugged the King's clever playboy, and both sobbed tears of joy over their miraculous reunion.

In between bouts of sobbing, the man was able to ask her. "O dear, dear mother, where are you living now?"

"I live next door," she said, "in the royal priest's mansion. Night and day I serve his young woman. Her beauty is without equal, like the mermaids sailors love to praise."

He asked, "Where are you going now, mother?"

"I'm going shopping for her perfumes and cosmetics, my son."

"There's no need, mother," he said, "from now on I will give you the best perfumes and cosmetics free of charge!" So he gave them to her, along with a bouquet of lovely flowers.

When the priest's lady saw all these, much better quality than usual, she asked why the priest was so happy with her.

"No, no," said the serving woman, "these are not from the priest. I got them at my son's shop." From then on she got perfumes and cosmetics from the playboy's shop, and kept the priest's money.

After a while the playboy began the next part of his plan. He pretended to be sick and stayed in bed.

When the servant came to the shop she asked, "Where is my son?" She was told he was too sick to work, and was taken to see him. She began massaging his back and asked, "What happened to you, my son?"

He replied, "Even if I were about to die, I couldn't tell you, my mother."

She continued, "If you can't tell me, whom can you tell?"

Then according to his plan, he broke down and admitted to her, "I was fine until you told me about your beautiful mistress – 'like the mermaids sailors love to praise'. Because of your description, I have fallen in love with her. I must have her. I can't live without her. I'm so depressed, without her I'll surely die!"

Then the woman said, "Don't worry, my son, leave it up to me." She took even more perfumes and cosmetics to the priest's lady. She said to her, "My lady, after my son heard from me about your beauty, he fell madly in love with you! I don't know what to do next!"

Since the priest was the only man she had ever seen, the lady was curious. And of course she resented being locked up by force. So she said, "If you can sneak him into my room, it's all right with me!"

Everything the servant took in and out was searched by the woman guards at the seven gates. So she had to have a plan. She swept up all the dust and dirt she could find in the whole mansion. Then she began taking some of it out each day in a large covered flower basket. Whenever she was searched, she made sure some of the dust and dirt got on the guard women's faces. This made them sneeze and cough. Pretty soon they stopped searching her when she went in and out.

Finally one day she hid the playboy in her covered flower basket. He was trim and fit, not heavy at all. She was able to sneak him past all seven guarded gates, and into the priest's lady's private chamber. The two lovers stayed together for several days and nights. So the playboy was able to destroy her perfect faithfulness, which had been forced on her by the cold-hearted priest.

Eventually she told him it was time to go. He said, "I will go. But first, since the old priest has been so mean to you, let me give him one good blow on the head!" She agreed and hid him in a closet. This too was part of his secret plan.

When the priest arrived, his lady said, "My lord and master, I'm so happy today! I'd like to dance while you play the guitar."

The priest said, "Of course, my beauty."

"But I'm too shy to dance in front of you," she added, "so please wear this blindfold while I dance." Again he agreed to her request and she put a blindfold over his eyes.

The priest played a pretty tune on his complicated Indian guitar, while his lady danced. After a bit she said, "As part of my dance, won't you let me give you a tap on the head?"

"As you wish, my dear," he said.

Then she motioned to the playboy, who came out of the closet, sneaked up from behind, and hit the old priest on the head! His eyes nearly popped out, and a bump began rising from the blow. He cried out and the lady put her hand in his. He said, "Such a soft hand sure can deliver a wallop, my dear!"

The playboy returned to the closet. The lady removed the priest's blindfold and put some ointment on his bump. When he had left, the serving woman hid the playboy in her flower basket and smuggled him out of the mansion. He went immediately to the King and told him the whole story, in a very boastful way, of course.

The next day the royal priest went to the palace as usual. The King said, "Shall we gamble on the throw of the dice?" The priest, expecting to win once more, agreed. Just as before, the King recited his lucky charm:

"If tempted, any woman will, for sure, give up her faithfulness and act impure."

As usual the priest added:

"Except my woman – faithful evermore!"

But lo and behold the dice fell in the King's favour and he took the priest's money.

The King said, "O priest, your woman is no exception! True faithfulness cannot be forced! Your plan was to snatch a newborn baby girl, lock her up behind seven gates guarded by seven guards, and force her to be good. But you have failed. Any prisoner's greatest wish is freedom!

"She blindfolded you and then her playboy lover gave you that bump on your old bald head – which proves your gates and guards were useless!"

The priest returned home and accused his lady. But in the meantime, she had come up with a plan of her own. She said, "No, no, my lord, I have been completely faithful to you. No man has ever touched me except you! And I will prove it in a trial by fire. I will walk on fire without being burned to prove I speak the truth."

She ordered the old servant woman to fetch her son, the playboy. She was to tell him to take the lady by the hand and prevent her from stepping in the flames. This the woman did.

On the day of the trial by fire, the priest's lady said to the crowd of onlookers, "I have never been touched by any man except this priest, my master. By this truth, may the fire have no power over me."

Then, just as she was about to step into the fire, the playboy leaped from the crowd and grabbed her hand. He shouted, "Stop! Stop! How can this priest be so cruel as to force this tender young lady into a raging fire!"

She shook her hand free and said to the priest, "My lord, since this man has touched my hand, the trial by fire is useless. But you can see my good intention!"

The priest realised he had been tricked. He beat her as he drove her away forever. At last she was free of him, and mistress of her own fate.

28. THE KING WHO KNOWS THE LANGUAGE OF ANIMALS

Once upon a time, when the Bodhisattva was Sakka, Senaka was the King of Benares. The King Senaka was friendly with a certain Naga King. This Naga King, they say, left the Naga world and ranged the earth seeking food. The village boys seeing him said, "This is a snake," and struck him with clods and other things.

The King, going to amuse himself in his garden, saw them, and being told they were beating a snake, said, "Don't let them beat him. Drive them away." And this was done.

So the Naga King got his life, and when he went back to the Naga world, he took many jewels, and coming at midnight to the King's bedchamber he gave them to him, saying, "I got my life through you." So he made friendship with the King and came again and again to see him. He appointed one of his Naga girls, insatiate in pleasures, to be near the King and protect him, and he gave the King a charm, saying, "If ever you do not see her, repeat this charm."

One day the King went to the garden with the Naga girl and was amusing himself in the lotus tank. The Naga girl seeing a water snake quitted her human shape and misconducted with him. The King not seeing the girl said, "Where is she gone?" and repeated the spell. Then he saw her in her misconduct and struck her with a piece of bamboo.

She went in anger to the Naga world, and when she was asked, "Why are you come?" she said, "Your friend struck me on the back because I did not do his bidding," showing the mark of the blow.

The Naga King, not knowing the truth, called four Naga youths and sent them with orders to enter Senaka's bedchamber and destroy him like chaff by the breath of their nostrils. They entered the chamber at the royal bedtime.

As they came in, the King was saying to the Queen, "Lady, do you know where the Naga girl has gone?"

"King, I do not," the Queen replied.

"Today when we were bathing in the tank, she quitted her shape and misconducted herself with a water snake. I said, 'Don't do that,' and struck her with a piece of bamboo to give her a lesson. And now I fear she may have gone to the Naga world and told some lie to my friend, destroying his goodwill to me."

The young Nagas hearing this turned back at once to the Naga world and told their King what they had heard. He being moved went instantly to the King's chamber, told him all and was forgiven. Then he said, "In this way I make amends," and gave the King a charm giving knowledge of all sounds. "This, O King, is a priceless spell. If you give anyone this spell you will at once enter the fire and die."

The King said, "It is well," and accepted it. From that time he understood the voice even of ants.

One day he was sitting on the dais eating solid food with honey and molasses, and a drop of honey, a drop of molasses, and a morsel of cake fell on the ground. An ant seeing this came crying, "The King's honey jar is broken on the dais, his molasses cart and cake cart are upset. Come and eat honey and molasses and cake."

The King hearing the cry laughed. The Queen being near him thought, "What has the King seen that he laughs?"

When the King had eaten his solid food and bathed and sat down cross-legged, a fly said to his wife, "Come, lady, let us enjoy love."

She said, "Excuse me for a little, husband. They will soon be bringing perfumes to the King. As he perfumes himself some powder will fall at his feet. I will stay there and become fragrant, then we will enjoy ourselves lying on the King's back."

The King hearing the voice laughed again. The Queen thought again, "What has he seen that he laughs?"

Again when the King was eating his supper, a lump of rice fell on the ground. The ants cried, "A wagon of rice has broken in the King's palace, and there is none to eat it."

The King hearing this laughed again. The Queen took a golden spoon and helping him reflected, "Is it at the sight of me that the King laughs?"

She went to the bedchamber with the King and at bedtime she asked, "Why did you laugh, O King?"

He said, "What have you to do with why I laugh?" But being asked again and again her told her.

Then she said, "Give me your spell of knowledge."

He said, "It cannot be given." But though repulsed she pressed him again.

The King said, "If I give you this spell, I shall die."

"Even though you die, give it to me."

The King, being in the power of womankind, saying, "It is well," consented and went to the park in a chariot, saying, "I shall enter the fire after giving away this spell."

At that moment Sakka, King of gods, looked down on the earth and seeing this case said, "This foolish King, knowing that he will enter the fire through womankind, is on the way; I will give him his life."

So he took Suja, daughter of the Asuras, and went to Benares. He became a he-goat and made her a she-goat, and resolving that the people should not see them, he stood before the King's chariot. The King and the Sindh asses yoked in the chariot saw him, but none else saw him. For the sake of starting talk he was as if making love with the she-goat.

One of the Sindh asses yoked in the chariot seeing him said, "Friend goat, we have heard before, but not seen, that goats are stupid and shameless. But you are doing, with all of us looking on, this thing that should be done in

secret and in a private place, and are you not ashamed? What we have heard before agrees with this that we see."

And so he spoke the first stanza:

"'Goats are stupid', says the wise man, and the words are surely true: This one knows not he's parading what in secret he should do."

The goat hearing him spoke two stanzas:

"O sir donkey, think and realize your own stupidity. You're tied with ropes, your jaw is wrenched, and very downcast is your eye.

"When you're loosened, you don't escape, sir, that's a stupid habit too. And that Senaka you carry, he's more stupid still than you."

The King understood the talk of both animals, and hearing it he quickly sent away the chariot. The ass hearing the goat's talk spoke the fourth stanza:

"Well sir, King of goats, you fully know my great stupidity. But how Senaka is stupid. Please do explain to me."

The goat explaining this spoke the fifth stanza:

"He who his own special treasure on his wife will throw away, cannot keep her faithful ever and his life he must betray."

The King hearing his words said, "King of goats, you will surely act for my advantage. Tell me now what is right for me to do."

Then the goat said, "King, to all animals no one is dearer than self. It is not good to destroy oneself and abandon the honour one has gained for the sake of anything that is dear." So he spoke the sixth stanza:

"A King, like thee, may have conceived desire and yet renounced it if his life's the cost. Life is the chief thing. What can man seek higher? If life's secured, desires need never be crossed."

So the Bodhisattva exhorted the King. The King, delighted, asked, "King of goats, whence come you?"

"I am Sakka, O King, come to save you from death out of pity for you."

"King of gods, I promised to give her the charm. What am I to do now?"

"There is no need for the ruin of both of you. You say, 'It is the way of the craft,' and have her beaten with some blows. By this means she will not get it."

The King said, "It is well," and agreed. The Bodhisattva after exhortation to the King went to Sakka's heaven. The King went to the garden, had the Queen summoned and then said, "Lady, will you have the charm?"

"Yes, lord."

"Then go through the usual custom."

"What custom?"

"A hundred stripes on the back, but you must not make a sound."

She consented through greed for the charm. The King made his slaves take whips and beat her on both sides. She endured two or three stripes and then cried, "I don't want the charm."

The King said, "You would have killed me to get the charm," and so flogging the skin off her back he sent her away. After that she could not bear to talk of it again.

🐘 🐘 🐘

29. THE PEARL NECKLACE

When King Brahmadatta was ruling in Benares, the Bodhisattva became one of his ministers after completing his education.

One day the King went on an outing to his pleasure garden. A big crowd from the court went with him. They visited many parts of the lovely park. Near a cool forest they came upon a beautiful clear pond. The King decided to go for a swim. So he dove into the water. Then he invited all the ladies of his harem to join him in the refreshing pond.

Laughing together, the harem women took off all their ornaments and jewellery - from their heads, necks, ears, wrists, fingers, waists, ankles and toes. Along with their outer clothing, they handed all these over to their servant girls for safekeeping. Then they jumped into the pond with King Brahmadatta.

The King had given one of his favourite Queens a very valuable pearl necklace. She was so fond of it that she called it by a pet name, 'Most Precious'.

It just so happened that a curious she-monkey had been watching all this from a branch of a nearby tree. Peering between the green leaves, she had paid very close attention. When she had caught sight of the Most Precious pearl necklace, her eyes had nearly popped out of her head!

Imagining how grand she would look wearing the Queen's beautiful necklace, she patiently watched the servant girl who was guarding it. In the beginning the girl watched very carefully. But the heat of the day soon made her drowsy. When the she-monkey saw her start to snooze, she swung down from the tree as fast as the wind. In a flash she grabbed the necklace called Most Precious, put it around her neck, and ran back up the tree.

Afraid that the other monkeys would see it, the little thief hid the gleaming pearl necklace in a hollow of the tree. Then she sat guarding her loot, remaining silent and pretending to be as innocent as a nun!

In a minute or two the servant girl awoke from her accidental nap. Frightened, she immediately looked over

the Queen's possessions. When she saw the necklace was missing she yelled out in terror, "Help! Help! Some man has taken the Queen's pearl necklace, the one called Most Precious!"

After running to her side, security guards went and reported the theft to the King. He ordered them to stop at nothing, and to catch the thief immediately. Frightened of the King's wrath, the guards began dashing madly around the pleasure garden searching for the thief.

At that very moment there happened to be a poor man walking just outside the garden. He was on his way back to his far-off home village after paying his meagre taxes to the royal treasury. The commotion from inside the park scared him and he started running away.

Unfortunately, the security guards saw him running and said to each other, "That must be the thief!" They rushed through the garden gate and after a short chase easily captured the innocent man. They began beating him as they shouted, "You no good thief! Confess that you robbed the Queen's pearl necklace, the one she calls Most Precious."

The poor man thought, "If I say I didn't take it, these men will beat me to death for sure. But if I confess, they will have to take me to the King." So he said, "Yes, I admit it, I took the necklace." Hearing this the security guards handcuffed him and hauled him off to the King.

After being told of the man's confession, the King asked him, "Where is the Most Precious necklace now? What have you done with it?"

Being a somewhat clever fellow, the prisoner replied, "My Lord King, I am a very poor man indeed. I have never in my life owned anything at all valuable, not a Most Precious bed or a Most Precious chair, and certainly not a Most Precious pearl necklace. It was Your Majesty's own Chief Financial Adviser who made me steal this Most Precious. I gave it to him. He alone knows where it is now."

King Brahmadatta summoned his Chief Financial Adviser and asked, "Did you take Most Precious from this man's hands?"

"Yes my lord," said he.

"Where is it now?" asked the King.

"I gave it to the Royal Teacher Priest."

The Royal Teacher Priest was called for and asked about the stolen necklace. He claimed, "I gave it to the Official Court Musician."

He in turn was summoned and questioned. He answered, "I gave Most Precious to a high class prostitute."

When she was identified and brought to the King, he demanded to know what she had done with the Queen's pearl necklace. But she alone replied, "Your Majesty, I don't know anything about a pearl necklace!"

As the sun began to set, the King said, "Let us continue this investigation tomorrow." He handed the five suspects over to his ministers and returned to his palace for the night.

30. THE WISE MINISTER

The royal minister who happened to be the Bodhisattva, realized that the mystery could be solved only by careful examination. Jumping to conclusions could lead to the wrong answers. So he started examining and analyzing the situation in his mind.

He thought, "The necklace was lost inside the pleasure garden. But the poor villager was captured outside the pleasure garden. The gates had strong guards standing watch. Therefore, the villager could not have come in to steal the necklace. Likewise, no one from inside the garden could have gotten out through the guarded gates with the stolen necklace. So it can be seen that none of these people could have gotten away with Most Precious, either from inside or outside!

"What a mystery! The poor man who was first accused must have said he gave it to the Chief Financial Adviser just to save himself. The Chief Financial Adviser must have thought it would go easier for him if the Royal Teacher Priest were involved. The priest must have blamed the Official Court Musician so that music would make their time in the palace dungeon pass more pleasantly. And the Official Court Musician probably thought that being with the high class prostitute would take away the misery of prison life. So he said he gave the necklace to her.

"After examining carefully, it is easy to see that all five suspects must be innocent. But the garden is full of monkeys who are known to cause mischief. No doubt some she-monkey thought Most Precious would set her above the rest, and the necklace is still in her hands."

So he went to the King and said, "Your Excellency, if you hand over the suspects to me, I will do the investigation for you."

"By all means, my wise minister," said the King, "examine into it yourself."

The minister called for his servant boys. He told them to keep the five suspects together in one place. They were to hide nearby, listen to all that was said, and then report back to him.

When the five prisoners thought they were alone they began talking freely to each other. First the Chief Financial Adviser said to the poor villager, "You little crook! We

never saw each other before. So when did you give the stolen Most Precious to me?"

He replied, "My lord sir, most exalted adviser to the great King, I have never had anything of any value whatsoever, not even a broken down bed or chair. I certainly have not seen any such Most Precious necklace! I don't know what you people are talking about. Being scared to death by the King's guards, I only mentioned you in the hope that one as important as you could free us both. Please, my lord, don't be angry at me."

The Royal Teacher Priest said to the Chief Financial Adviser. "You see, this man admits he has not given it to you, so how could you have given it to me?"

He replied, "We are both in high positions. I thought that if we got together and backed each other up, we could settle this matter."

The Official Court Musician asked, "O Royal Teacher Priest, when did you give the Queen's pearl necklace to me?"

"I thought that if you were imprisoned with me," said the priest, "your music would make it much more pleasant. That's why I lied."

Then the woman said to the Official Court Musician, "You miserable crook! When did I come to you? When did you come to me? We have never met each other before. So when could you possibly have given me the stolen Most Precious?"

He said to her, "O dear young lady, please don't be angry with me. I only accused you so that when we five are imprisoned together, your being with us will make us all happy."

Not being either a poor frightened stranger or a slippery government official, the high class prostitute was the only one who had told the truth. So there was no one to accuse her of shifting the blame.

Of course the wise minister's servants had been eavesdropping on the entire conversation. When they reported it all back to him, he realized his suspicion was confirmed – some she-monkey must have taken the necklace. So he thought, "I must come up with a plan to get it back."

First he had a bunch of cheap imitation jewel ornaments made. Then he had several she-monkeys captured in the royal pleasure garden. He had them decorated with the imitation ornaments - necklaces on their necks and bracelets on their wrists and ankles. Then they were released in the garden. The minister ordered his servants to watch all the she-monkeys carefully. If they saw anyone with the missing pearl necklace, they were to scare her into dropping it.

The she-monkey who had taken Most Precious was still guarding it in the hollow of the tree. The other she-monkeys strutted back and forth saying, "See how fine we look. We have these beautiful necklaces and bracelets."

She couldn't stand seeing and hearing this. She thought, "Those are nothing but worthless imitations." To show them all up, she put around her own neck the Most Precious necklace of real pearls.

Immediately the servants frightened her into dropping it. They took it to their master, the wise minister. He took it to the King and said, "Your Majesty, here is the pearl necklace, the one called Most Precious. None of the five who admitted to the crime was really a thief. It was taken instead by a greedy little she-monkey living in your pleasure garden."

The amazed King asked, "How did you find out it was taken by a she-monkey? And how did you get it back?" The minister told the whole story.

The King said, "You were certainly the right one for the job. In times of need, it is the wise who are appreciated most." Then he rewarded him by showering him with wealth, like a heavy rain of the seven valuables - gold, silver, pearls, jewels, lapis lazuli, diamonds and coral.

31. THE WISE PRINCE

O nce upon a time, the Bodhisattva was born as the last of King Brahmadatta's 100 sons and grew up to be a wise young man.

In those days there were Silent Buddhas who came to the palace to receive alms food. They were called Buddhas because they were enlightened – they knew the Truth and experienced life as it really is, in every present moment. They were called Silent because they did not preach the Truth. This was because they knew it was a time when no one would be able to understand it. However, being filled with sympathy for the unhappiness of all beings, the Silent Buddhas wished to help anyone who asked them.

One day the young prince was thinking about his ninety-nine elder brothers and wondering if he had any chance to become King of Benares. He decided to ask the Silent Buddhas about it.

The next day the Silent Buddhas came as usual to collect alms food in the palace. The prince brought purified water and washed their feet. When they had sat down he gave them appetizers to eat. Before giving the next course he said to them, "I am hundredth in line to the throne. What are the odds that I will become King of Benares?"

They replied, "O prince, with so many older brothers there is almost no chance you will ever be King here. However, you might become King of Takshasila. If you can get there in seven days you can become King. But on your way there is a dangerous forest. You must take the road passing through it, since it would take twice as long to go around it.

"That forest is known as 'Devils Woods', because it is filled with all kinds of devils – he-devils, she-devils, and even little children-devils! The she-devils spend most of their time by the roadside. They use magic to make buildings and entire cities appear along the way.

"The buildings have ceilings decorated with stars, and gorgeous rich couches surrounded by silk curtains of many colours. Sitting on these couches, the she-devils make themselves look like the sweetest, most pleasant of all goddesses. With words dripping like honey they attract travellers saying, 'You look tired. Come in, sit down, have something to drink and then be on your way.'

"Those who are persuaded to come in are invited to sit down. Then the strangers are killed by the she-devils and eaten while their blood is still hot!

"In this way those who are attracted by sight are trapped by the physical forms of women. Those who are attracted by sound are trapped by their singing voices and music. Those attracted by smell are trapped by the divine perfumes they wear. Those attracted by taste are trapped by the heavenly tasting delicacies they offer. Those attracted by touch are trapped by their soft luxurious beds and velvet couches.

"But if you, fair prince, can control all five senses, and force yourself to avoid looking at those beautiful enticing she-devils, only then can you become King of Takshasila in seven days."

The grateful Bodhisattva replied, "Thank you venerable ones, I will follow your advice. After hearing such warnings, how could I take the chance of looking at them?"

Then he asked the Silent Buddhas to give him special charms to protect him on his dangerous journey through Devils Woods. So they chanted protective blessings onto a string and some sand. He accepted the charms and paid his farewell respects to them, and then to his royal parents.

Returning to his own home he announced to his household servants, "I am going to Takshasila to win the Kingship. You are to remain here."

But five of them said, "We also wish to go with you."

"No," said he, "you can't come with me. I have been warned that on the way there are beautiful she-devils who trap people who can't resist the desires coming from their own five senses. Then they kill their victims and eat them while their blood is still hot. It is far too dangerous for you. I will rely only on myself and travel alone."

But the five would not listen. They said, "If we go with you, O prince, we will force ourselves to keep from looking at those beautiful she-devils. We will accompany you to Takshasila."

"If you insist, then so be it," said the prince, "but keep your determination strong."

The she-devils were waiting for them in Devils Woods. They had already magically formed beautiful villages and cities with lovely houses and palaces along the way.

It just so happened that one of the prince's five servants was easily enchanted by the sight of the curves and figures of the bodies of women. So he began to fall behind in order to admire them. The worried prince asked, "Why do you delay, my friend?"

"My feet ache," said the man, "let me sit and rest a while in one of these mansions. Then I will catch up with you."

"My good friend," said the prince, "those are she-devils. Don't chase after them!"

Nevertheless, blinded by the temptation of the sense of sight, the man replied, "My lord, I can't turn away.

Whatever will happen, let it happen!" Giving him one last warning, the prince continued on with the other four.

The one who remained behind went closer to the beautiful looking forms he was so attracted to. The she-devils killed him too and ate him on the spot!

Then they went farther into Devils Woods and created another mirage of a beautiful mansion. They sat inside and began singing the sweetest melodies, accompanied by the lovely sounds of all kinds of musical instruments. One of the prince's followers was enchanted by the sound of beautiful music. So he too fell behind and was gobbled up by the still hungry she-devils.

Farther down the road they created another magic mansion filled with the scents of all kinds of divine perfumes. This time the man who loved sweet smells fell behind and was eaten as well.

Next the she-devils created a fabulous restaurant filled with foods having the most heavenly flavours. Here the lover of the tastes of the finest delicacies wandered in and was devoured in turn.

Then the she-devils went still farther down the road, created soft luxurious beds and velvet couches, and sat on them. The last of the prince's followers was one who loved the touch of the softest fabrics and the most luxurious comfort. So he too fell behind and met his death, and was quickly eaten by the ravenous she-devils.

These events left the Bodhisattva all alone in Devils Woods. A certain she-devil thought, "Aha! This one is very strong-minded indeed. But I am even more determined. I will not stop until I have tasted his flesh!" So she alone stubbornly followed him, even though the other she-devils gave up the chase.

As she got closer to the edge of Devils Woods, some woodsmen saw her and asked. "Lovely lady, who is it that walks on ahead of you?"

"We are newlyweds," replied the lying demon, "he is my too pure husband, who ran away from me on our wedding night. That's why I'm chasing after him."

The woodsmen caught up to the prince and asked, "Noble sir, this delicate flower-like golden-skinned young maiden has left her family to live with you. Why don't you walk with her, instead of making her chase after you?"

The prince replied, "Good people, she is not my wife. She is a devil. She killed the five men who followed me and ate them while their blood was still hot!"

Whereupon the lovely looking devil said, "See how it is, gentlemen, anger can make husbands call their own wives devils and hungry ghosts! Such is the way of the world."

Continuing to follow the prince, the determined she-devil magically made herself look pregnant. Then she seemed to be a first-time mother carrying her make-believe baby on her hip. Whoever saw the pair questioned them just as the woodsmen had. Each time the Bodhisattva repeated, "She is not my wife. She is a devil. She killed the five men who followed me and ate them while their blood was still hot!"

32. THE FOOLISH KING

When they arrived at Takshasila, the she-devil made her 'son' disappear and followed alone. At the city gate the prince stopped and went into a rest house. Because of the magic power of the charmed sand and string he had gotten from the Silent Buddhas, the she-devil was not able to follow him inside. She stayed outside and made herself look as beautiful as a goddess.

The King of Takshasila happened to see her as he was going to his pleasure garden. Overwhelmed by her beauty, he decided he must have her. He sent a servant to ask if she was married. When he did so, she replied, "Yes, my husband is inside this rest house."

Hearing this, the prince called out from within, "She is not my wife. She is a devil. She killed the five men who followed me and ate them while their blood was still hot!" And once again she said, "See how it is, sir, anger can make husbands call their own wives devils and hungry ghosts! Such is the way of the world."

The servant returned to the King and told him what both of them had said. To which the King replied,

'Unowned goods belong to the King." So he sent for the she-devil and seated her on a royal elephant. After the procession returned to the palace, he made her his number one Queen.

That evening the King had a shampoo and bath, ate his supper, and went to bed. The demon had her supper, made herself look even more beautiful than before and followed the King to his bed. After pleasing him, she turned on her side and began to weep.

The King asked, "Why are you crying, my sweetheart?"

"My lord," said she, "you picked me up from the roadside. In this palace there are many jealous women. They will say, 'She has no mother or father, no family or country. She was found on the side of the road.' Don't let them make fun of me like that, my lord. Give me power over the whole Kingdom so none will dare challenge me."

"My lovely," replied the King, "I have no such power over the whole Kingdom. My authority is only over those who revolt or break the law." But since he was so pleased by her physical charms, the King continued, "My sweetheart, I will grant you complete authority over all who dwell within my palace."

Satisfied with this, the new Queen waited until the King was asleep. Then she secretly ran off to her home in the city of devils. She gathered together the she-devils, he-devils, and even the hungry little children-devils. Then she took them all back to the palace. She killed her new husband, the King, and gobbled him up - all except his bones! The other devils ate all the rest who lived in the palace - even the dogs and chickens! Only bones were left behind.

The next morning the people found the palace doors locked. Worried, they broke through the windows with axes, went inside, and found human heads and bones scattered around. Only then did they realize that the man in the rest house was right, that the King's new Queen was a flesh-eating devil.

Meanwhile, the Bodhisattva had protected himself from the murderous she-devil during the night. He had spread the charmed sand on the roof of the rest house

and wound the charmed string around the outside walls. At dawn he was still awake inside, standing alertly with sword in hand.

After cleaning up the mess in the palace the citizens discussed the situation among themselves. They said, "The man in the rest house must be master of his senses, since he did not even look at the she-devil's dangerous beauty. If such a noble, determined and wise man were ruling our country, we all would prosper. Let us make him our new King."

In unanimous agreement they went to the rest house and invited the prince to be their King. When he accepted, they escorted him to the palace, seated him on a pile of jewels, and crowned him King.

He ruled righteously, following the ten rules of good government. He avoided the four ways of going astray— prejudice, anger, fearfulness and foolishness. And he always remembered the advice of the Silent Buddhas, that had led him to the Kingship. Unlike his five unfortunate followers, he had resisted the blind desire for the pleasure of the five senses. Only then could he benefit all his subjects with his wise rule.

33. MAGHA THE GOOD

Once upon a time, there was a young noble called 'Magha the Good'. He lived in a remote village of just 30 families. When he was young, his parents married him to a girl who had qualities of character similar to his own. They were very happy together, and she gave birth to several children.

The villagers came to respect Magha the Good because he always tried to improve the village, for the good of all. Because they respected him, he was able to teach the five steps of training, to purify their thoughts, words and deeds.

Magha's way of teaching was by doing. An example of this happened one day when the villagers gathered to do handicraft work. Magha the Good cleaned a place for himself to sit, but before he could sit down, someone else sat there. So he patiently cleaned another place. Again a neighbour sat in his place. This happened over and over again, until he had patiently cleaned sitting places for all those present. Only then he could sit in the last place.

By using such examples of patience, Magha the Good taught his fellow villagers how to co-operate with each other, without quarrelling. Working together in this way, they constructed several buildings and made other improvements that benefited the whole village. Seeing the worthwhile results of patience and co-operation, based on following the gentle ways of the Five Training Steps, all in the village became calmer and more peaceful.

A natural side effect was that former crimes and wrong-doing completely disappeared!

You would think this would make everybody happier. However, there was one man who did not like the new situation at all. He was the head of the village, the politician who cared only about his own position.

Formerly, when there were murders and thefts, he handed out punishments. This increased his position of authority, and caused the villagers to fear him. When husbands or wives had affairs with others, the head man collected fines. In the same way, when reputations were damaged by lies, or contracts were not lived up to, he also collected fines. He even got tax money from the profits of selling strong liquor. He did not mind that drunkenness led to many of the crimes.

It is easy to see why the head man was upset to lose so much respect and power and money, due to the people living peacefully together. So he went to the King and said, "My lord, some of the remote villages are being robbed and looted by bandits. We need your help."

The King said, "Bring all these criminals to me."

The dishonest politician rounded up the heads of all 30 families and brought them as prisoners to the King. Without questioning them, the King ordered that they all be trampled to death by elephants.

All 30 were ordered to lie down in the palace courtyard and the elephants were brought in. They realized they were about to be trampled to death.

Magha the Good said to them, "Remember and concentrate on the peacefulness and purity that come from following the Five Training Steps, so you may feel loving-kindness towards all. In this way, do not get angry at the unjust King, the lying head man, or the unfortunate elephants."

The first elephant was brought in by his mahout. But when he tried to force him to trample the innocent villagers, the elephant refused. He trumpeted as he went away. Amazingly, this was repeated with each of the King's elephants. None would step on them.

The mahouts complained to the King that this was not their fault. "It must be," they said, "that these men have some drug that is confusing the elephants."

The King had the villagers searched, but they found nothing. Then his advisers said, "These men must be magicians who have cast an evil spell on your mighty elephants!"

The villagers were asked, "Do you have such a spell?"

Magha the Good said, "Yes, we do."

This made the King very curious. So he himself asked Magha, "What is this spell and how does it work?"

Magha the Good replied, "My lord King, we do not cast the same kinds of spells that others cast. We cast the spell of loving-kindness with minds made pure by following the Five Training Steps."

"What are these Five Training Steps?" asked the King.

Magha the Good said, "All of us have given up the five unwholesome actions, which are: destroying life, taking what is not given, doing wrong in sexual ways, speaking falsely, and losing one's mind from alcohol.

"In this way we have become harmless, so that we can give the gift of fearlessness to all. Therefore, the elephants lost their fear of the mahouts, and did not wish to harm us. They departed, trumpeting triumphantly. This was our protection, which you have called a 'spell'."

Finally seeing the wholesomeness and wisdom of these people, the King questioned them and learned the truth. He decided to confiscate all the property of the dishonest village head man and divide it among them.

The villagers were then free to do even more good works for the benefit of the whole village. Soon they began to build a big roadside inn, right next to the highway crossroads.

This was the biggest project they had yet undertaken. The men were confident because they had learned so well how to co-operate with each other for a common goal. But they had not yet learned how to co-operate in this work with the women of the village. They seemed to think it was 'man's work'.

By this time Magha the Good had four wives. Their names were Good-doer, Beauty, Happy and Well-born. Of these, the first wife, Good-doer, was the wisest. She wanted to pave the way for the women to benefit from co-operating in doing good work. So she gradually became friendly with the boss in charge of the roadside inn project.

Because she wanted to contribute by helping in a big way, she gave a present to the boss. She asked him, "Can you think of a way that I may become the most important contributor to this good work?"

The boss replied, "I know just such a way!" Then he secretly constructed the most important part of the building, the roof beam that would hold the roof together. He wrapped it up and hid it with Good-doer, so it could dry for the time necessary to become rigid and strong. Meanwhile, the men of the village continued happily in the building project. At last they got to the point of installing the roof beam. They began to make one, but the boss interrupted them. He said, "My friends, we cannot use fresh green wood to make the roof beam. It will bend and sag. We must have an aged dry roof beam. Go find one!"

When they searched in the village, they found that Good-doer just happened to have a perfect roof beam. It was even the right size! When they asked if they could buy it from her, she said, "It is not for sale at any price. I wish to contribute the roof beam for free, but only if you let me participate in building the inn."

The men were afraid to change their successful ways. So they said, "Women have never been part of this project. This is impossible."

Then they returned to the construction boss and told him what had happened. He said, "Why do you keep the women away? Women are part of everything in this world. Let us be generous and share the harmony and wholesomeness of this work with the women. Then the project and our village will be even more successful."

So they accepted the roof beam from Good-doer, and she helped to finish the building of the inn. Then Beauty had a wonderful garden built next to the inn, which she donated. It had all kinds of flowers and fruit trees. So too, Happy had a lovely pond dug, and planted beautiful lotuses in it. But Well-born, being the youngest and a little spoiled, did nothing for the inn.

In the evenings, Magha the Good held meetings in the roadside inn. He taught the people to assist their parents and elders, and to give up harsh words, accusing others behind their backs, and being stingy.

It is said that the lowest heaven world contains the gods of the four directions, North, East, South and West. Because he followed his own teachings, Magha the Good died with happiness in his heart. He was reborn as Sakka, King of the second lowest heaven world.

In time, the heads of all the other families of the village, as well as Good-doer, Beauty and Happy, also died. They were reborn as gods under King Sakka. This was known as the 'Heaven of 33'.

34. SAKKA AND ASURAS

So very long ago, there were some unfortunate ugly gods called 'Asuras'. They had taken to living in the second heaven world.

The one who had been Magha the Good in his previous life, was now Sakka, King of the Heaven of 33. He thought, "Why should we live in our Heaven of 33 with these unfortunate ugly Asuras? Since this is our world, let us live happily by ourselves."

So he invited them to a party and got them drunk on very strong liquor. It seems that, in being reborn, King Sakka had forgotten some of his own teachings as Magha the Good. After getting the Asuras drunk, he got them to go to a lower world, just as big as the Heaven of 33.

When they sobered up and realized they had been tricked into going to a lower heaven world, the Asuras became angry. They rose up and made war against King Sakka. Soon they were victorious, and Sakka was forced to run away.

While retreating in his mighty war chariot, he came to the vast forest where the Garulas have their nests. These are gods who, unfortunately, have no super powers. Instead they are forced to get around by flapping huge heavy wings.

When King Sakka's chariot drove through their forest, it upset their nests and made the baby Garulas fall down. They cried in fear and agony. Hearing this, Sakka asked his charioteer where these sad cries were coming from.

He answered, "These are the shrieks of terror coming from the baby Garulas, whose nests and trees are being destroyed by your powerful war chariot."

Hearing this suffering, King Sakka realized that all lives, including his own, are only temporary. Hearing this suffering, the compassion of the Great Being, which passes from life to life, arose within him and said, "Let the little ones have no more fear. The first training step must not be broken. There can be no exception. I will not destroy even one life for the sake of a heavenly kingdom that must some day end. Instead I will offer my life to the victorious Asuras. Turn back the chariot!"

So the chariot returned in the direction of the Heaven of 33. The Asuras saw King Sakka turn around, and thought he must have reinforcements from other worlds. So they ran, without looking back, down to their lower heaven world.

35. SAKKA AND HIS FOURTH WIFE

King Sakka returned victoriously to his palace in the Heaven of 33. His fourth wife, Well-born, had died and been reborn as a slender crane in the forest. Since he missed her, Sakka found her and brought her up to the Heaven of 33 for a visit. He showed her the mansion and the garden and the pond of his three wives. He told her that, by doing good work, the other three had gained merit. This merit had brought them happiness, both in their previous lives and in their rebirths.

He said, "You, my dear crane, in your previous life as Well-born, did no such good work. So you did not gain either merit or happiness, and were reborn as a forest crane. I advise you to begin on the path of purity by following the Five Training Steps." After being taught the five steps, the lovely crane decided to follow them. Then she returned to the forest.

Not long afterwards, King Sakka was curious about how the crane was doing. So he took the shape of a fish and lay down in front of her. The crane picked him up by the head. She was just about to swallow the King of the Heaven of 33, when the fish wiggled his tail.

Immediately the crane thought, "This fish must be alive!" Remembering the first training step, she released the living fish back into the stream.

Rising from the water, King Sakka returned to his godly form and said, "It is very good, my dear crane, that

you are able to follow the Five Training Steps." Then he returned to the second heaven world.

In the fullness of time, the crane died. Following the Five Training Steps had brought her both merit and a peaceful mind. So she was reborn in the wonderful state of mankind, into a potter's family in Benares, in northern India.

Again King Sakka was interested in finding out where the one who had been Well-born, and then the crane, was now reborn. He found her in the potter's family, and wanted to help her in gaining merit and finding happiness.

So he disguised himself as an old man and created a cart full of golden cucumbers. He went into Benares and shouted, "Cucumbers! Cucumbers! I have cucumbers!"

When people came to buy these amazing cucumbers, he said, "These golden cucumbers are not for sale. I will give them away, but only to one who is wholesome, that is, one who follows the Five Training Steps."

The people said, "We have never heard of the Five Training Steps. But we will buy your golden cucumbers. Name your price!"

He repeated, "My cucumbers are not for sale. I have brought them to give to any person who practises the Five Training Steps."

The people said, "This man has come here only to play tricks on us." So they left him alone.

Soon Well-born heard about this unusual man. Even though she had been reborn, she still had the habit of following the Five Training Steps. So she thought, "This man must have come to find me."

She went to him and asked for the golden cucumbers.

He said, "Do you follow the Five Training Steps? Have you given up destroying life, taking what is not given, doing wrong in sexual ways, speaking falsely, and losing your mind from alcohol?"

She answered, "Yes sir, I do follow these steps, and I am peaceful and happy."

Then the old man said, "I brought these cucumbers especially for you, to encourage you to gain more merit and future happiness."

So he left the cart of golden cucumbers with her, and returned to the Heaven of 33.

Throughout the rest of her life, the woman was very generous with all this gold. Spreading her happiness among others, she gained merit. After she died, she was reborn as the daughter of the King of the Asuras. She grew up to be a goddess of great beauty. To the Asuras this seemed like a miracle, since the rest of them were the ugliest of all the gods.

The Asura King was pleased with his daughter's goodness, as well as her famous beauty. He gathered all the Asuras together and gave her the freedom to choose a husband.

Sakka, King of the Heaven of 33, knew of the latest rebirth of the one who had been his wife Well-born, then a crane, and then a potter's daughter. So he came down to the lower heaven world and took the shape of an ordinary ugly Asura. He thought, "If Well-born chooses a husband whose inner qualities of wholesomeness are the same as hers, we will be reunited at last!"

Because of her past associations with Magha the Good, reborn as King Sakka, now disguised as an ordinary Asura, the beautiful princess was drawn to him. So she picked him from among all the Asuras.

King Sakka took her to the Heaven of 33, made her his fourth wife, and they lived happily ever after.

卐 卐 卐